A LINE ONCE
CROSSED

{BOOK 3}

DD ANDER

www.ddander.com

ISBN:

978-0-9953193-9-4 (paperback)

978-0-9959821-0-9 (eBook)

TABLE OF CONTENTS

Prologue..ix

1. Richard's Story... 3

2. Claire Refuses To Hide 5

3. Two Can Play At This Game 7

MEANWHILE . . .

1. Erin Tells Her Story.. 13

2. We Had No Choice 19

3. O'malley Goes Sailing... 23

4. The Eulogy.. 25

5. Janice And Mikey Reconnect 27

6. Mikey Comes Clean 29

7. Derek's Take 31

8. The Time Has Come 33

9. Janice Rebooted.. 35

10. Mikey's Honour... 37

11. Mikey Goes To Church.. 39

12. Claire's Journey.. 41

13. Bon Voyage... 43

14. Mikey Has A Proposal... 47

15. On The Trail.. 51

16. Strangers In Our Home 53

17. And Away She Goes . . . Again.. 55

18. Erin And Janice And Joline.. 59

19.   Take It To The Judge 63

20.   You First, Gerald 65

21.   Table For 4 Please 69

22.   Claire Makes Her Move 71

23.   Derek Readies For The Storm 73

24.   Second Times A Charm 75

25.   Janice Goes To Bocas 77

26.   Erin And Sylvia 81

27.   Claire Makes Her Move 83

28.   Derek Sees His Lawyer 85

29.   Claire's Revenge 87

30.   Mikey's Missing Janice 91

31.   Derek Talks To Mikey And Rick 93

32.   The Alpha And The Pup 97

33.   Portland On The Phone 99

34.   But Mom, I Really, Really Like Him 101

35.   Mikey's Move 105

36.   Derek Confronts Claire 109

37.   Claire's Take 111

38.   Tell Me More About Abbas 113

39.   It's All About You, Doug 117

40.   What Now Derek? 119

41.   Alpha Dog No More 121

42.   Get Ready, Los Angeles 125

43.   Janice Heads Home 127

44. Millie Takes Charge 129

45. The Mol And The Cop 131

46. Your Move Abbas 133

47. Claire Meets Ethan 137

48. Between A Rock And A Hard Place 139

49. Doug And The Dog House 143

50. Gerald's Turn 145

51. Joline Makes A Decision 147

52. Derek Calls Ethan 149

53. Claire Feels The Heat 155

54. Claire Arranges To Pick Up Her Stuff 157

55. Unconditional Love 161

56. Be Careful Derek 163

57. Mikey's Conflicted 165

58. Joline Calls Mikey 167

59. Derek And Mikey Finally Meet 169

60. Go For It Mikey 173

61. Janice Calls Joline 177

62. Claire Puts On Her Armour 179

63. Mikey Contacts Derek 183

64. Ethan Makes The Arrangements 185

65. Mikey Heads To L.A. 187

66. Janice Heads For The Bistro 189

67. Peace River, Alberta, Canada 191

68. Claire And Mikey Have A Chat 195

69. Meanwhile Back In Seattle 197

70. Ethan's Story Expanded 199

71. Saturday In L.A. 201

72. We Have A Visitor...203

73. We Have A Fingerprint...207

74. Back In Seattle...211

75. Epilogue..213

76. DD ANDER's Bio 215

PROLOGUE

CLAIRE

THERE WERE NO FINGER PRINTS. Even the attached note had been wiped clean. The message was clear. YOU'RE A RAT! The note made it quite clear: And soon you'll be a dead one!

Claire had crossed a lot of people during her investigative career. And now it was payback time. And this was added: I lost everything! So will you!

And all she could think of was: thank God we don't have kids!

DEREK

Derek's career as a homicide detective with Seattle's finest was going great, but now Claire, his wife, was being stalked. In their own home, no less! Plus her brother Mikey couldn't decide which side of the law he wanted to operate on. And that was just the tip of the iceberg!

MIKEY

He loved Janice. But he'd walked away. He didn't want the woman he loved to suffer because of him. And now he knew who had attacked him and where they lived. But first he'd have to resign from the church. Pastor Rick refused to accept his resignation. But here's what he'd do. "I'll give you three months of unpaid leave. Then we need to talk! Don't do anything stupid!"

JANICE AND JOLINE

These two were tight. But it was time to have that mother, daughter talk. Joline saw it differently. It was time to have a woman to woman talk. "Remember Mom, I'm not a child anymore."

A LINE ONCE CROSSED

RICHARD'S STORY

"**Y**OU TOOK AWAY MY LIFE! And now I'm going to take away yours!" Richard could barely control the anger that welled within him. "God, are you going to pay!" He rubbed his hands together in anticipation of what was to come.

Claire had made a lot of enemies over her career. She had dared to take on cases that others deemed too dangerous. She was tenacious and unafraid; reckless, some would say. She didn't seem to care what happened to her. Just as long as she got the story.

And there were many convictions; and countless threats. From those currently under investigation, and from those whom the long arm of the law had finally placed in their protective custody. These were the more dangerous ones. Richard was one of the latter. Now he was a free man, and forgiveness had not touched this soulless man. But revenge had! And how sweet it would be! She'd taken away his freedom, and as a result he lost his family, his reputation, and he'd ended up penniless. Now it was her turn!

He liked the dead rat idea. And the note. He'd make her suffer like he had, and then one day, it would all be over. He had lived hell on earth, now it was her turn!

He began staking out her place the moment he walked out of that dungeon. "So you think you can just go on destroying people's lives with no consequences, hey?" Under his breath. "Well, get ready, lady.

3

This is going to be fun!" It took another week to ensure that his plan would work; no street cameras in the area; no dog at the house; no snoopy neighbours as far as he could tell; the tree lined streets should obscure his vehicle reasonably well; and it would only take a few seconds to deliver the package, ring the doorbell, and get the hell out of there.

The elevation on the street a block up from her place allowed the perfect vantage point. He could park the car; zoom in on the door with his camera, but still be far enough away not to attract attention. "Perfect. Now I'll just wait. She should be bursting through that door any second now." But she didn't. "What the hell?" She would've opened the package by now, surely to God!

Then he noticed another vehicle pulling into the driveway. "Hubby. This should be interesting." Again to himself. And then he heard the sirens, and shortly thereafter, both the ambulance and the police pulled into the driveway. "This is even better than I thought." He hung around until he saw her being taken out on the stretcher. "Perfect! Lady, this is just the beginning."

CLAIRE REFUSES TO HIDE

"WHAT AM I SUPPOSED TO DO? Hide under my bed? Ain't gonna happen!" Claire was peed. "If he thinks he can intimidate me, he picked the wrong chick!"

And that's what drove Derek nuts. God, was she stubborn. By the same token, he wouldn't want her on his case! But this guy was obviously pretty damn serious. He'd gone to a lot of trouble, and if that was any indication, there were a whole lot more surprises on the way.

And then her brother, Mikey, beat two gang members up so badly that they ended up in the hospital. And of course, they weren't talking. Nor was Mikey. He was at home at the time. He must've fallen asleep. Yeah right! These two apples had obviously fallen from the same tree. Geez!

So now he had a friend that he was trying to protect, despite himself, and a wife that seemed to have a death wish. Personally, he had a life wish and he'd like to fulfill it! And he'd like their company!

But if Richard had anything to say about it, Claire's lifeline wouldn't be growing much longer. "Time for part two. Get ready. I'm coming for you."

TWO CAN PLAY AT THIS GAME

THERE'D JUST BEEN THAT one incident so far so Claire began to relax, a little. Threats in her business were the norm, but this last one was a bit intense, so she wasn't taking it lightly. So she started making inquiries to see who had recently been released from prison that might be psychotic enough to carry out this kind of threat. More than likely, if she was getting threats, so were the trial judge, prosecutor, and often, their own lawyers. No harm in checking it out.

She'd been involved in investigative journalism for many years by now, and knew that stalking was a real problem. If you happened to be the one they fixated on, they could make your life a living hell. It was obvious that this individual had her in his sights.

Even trying to check on past cases was a crap shoot at best. But at least it was something. After going through dozens of past cases, Claire came across a couple of files that needed further investigation. She contacted the appropriate authorities to see if anyone else on any of the cases was being harassed. None. She was on her own. Great! But it was better than sitting around doing nothing.

She remembered the case well. He called himself "Doc." This dude was certainly capable of pulling something like this off. She remembered the first time she'd met him in person. A chill had run up her spine the moment they shook hands, and all she could think was "God, I wouldn't want to be alone anywhere with this guy!" She could tell he sensed her dislike, so he added a couple of vulgarities to ensure that she knew the feelings were mutual.

The police had hooked him in a sting operation involved in procuring underage girls and boys for "entertainment" purposes. They didn't have enough evidence to charge him with anything but a misdemeanour, but the cop in charge gave Claire a call anyway. His hands may have been tied, but he'd seen her work on other files. If he could get her interested, maybe she could dig up enough evidence to put this scumbag away for a very long time.

There were dozens of files like this one, but these guys were good at what they did. But this guy was cocky, and that was enough to get her attention. And abusing underage kids? This was a no brainer!

He didn't know what hit him. One day he was king of the roost; the next day he was in solitary confinement. For his own protection, no less. Even that couldn't stop the beatings he endured over several years. Unfortunately, he hadn't died in prison. He'd been out for several weeks now, and it wouldn't surprise her one bit if he was the creep. Time to check him out in person!

But that's when she got a call from Derek. "Hon, can you come down to the station? Now."

"Of course, what's up? What happened?"

"We'll talk when you get here. Bye." And with that he hung up.

Well, whatever it was, it sounded important so Claire headed down to the station. They ushered her in the moment she arrived; they seemed unusually solemn. Something was obviously up.

Derek beckoned her into his office, motioned her to sit. Serious, or what? "What's up? You'd think someone died or something. Oh God, did someone? Sorry!" Claire, just shut up. Please.

"I nearly did."

"What?"

"This morning. Driving to work as usual. Suddenly someone cut me off; I swerved and hit the brakes . . . there was none. I was clipping right along too. I tried gearing down, I even applied the emergency brake. Nothing. So I cut it to the right to try and get out of traffic but it was too busy. I had no choice but to go through the intersection on a red light. I nearly made it but the semi couldn't avoid me. He caught my right back end, spun me around, and fortunately I ended up in the ditch." He stopped for a moment, but then continued. "Claire, the brake lines had all been cut. It wasn't an accident."

Claire sat there in stunned silence. "Someone tried to kill you? Oh my God! Do you think it was my stalker? Are you okay?"

"I'm fine. A bit stiff, but that's it. I'm pretty damn sure it's the same guy! Claire, I'm worried about you."

Not that Claire could ever be accused of procrastination but it was time to confront "Doc" in person. In fact, she'd have a camera crew in tow. And that's what she did. They caught him coming out of a hardware store a couple of blocks from where he lived. And he was walking. Perfect!

"You can't talk to me. Get out of here! I'm calling the cops!" He was pissed.

"Go ahead. Do you need the number? I just have a few questions."

"Leave me alone!" He screamed at her. "This is harassment. I'm calling my lawyer. I'll sue your ass off!"

"For what, exactly? I'm just conducting a random person on the street interview. I just have one question: Do you think perverts should be locked up forever?" No answer. "Okay then, do you think we should have the death penalty for anyone convicted of trafficking underage kids? I'm sure you must have an opinion you'd like to share with all the parents out there.

What's that? Sorry, could you repeat that, please?" Claire wasn't about to let him off the hook that easy. "No comment? Ok. Thanks for your time."

Doc was livid. She wouldn't have been surprised to see him have a heart attack right there on the spot. But, no such luck. And besides, her gut told her he wasn't the one. He wasn't man enough to handle anyone but a bunch of vulnerable kids. And then to herself. "I'm going to put him away again. Mark my words."

Claire was expecting the call. Her boss wanted to have a little chat. In person. "Catch the next plane to Houston. Boardroom. 1 pm tomorrow."

"Here we go again. I shoulda cleared it with him first. Damn!"

MEANWHILE . . .

ERIN TELLS HER STORY

"**M**OM, DO YOU HAVE TIME to meet Erin and me for lunch? My treat." Joline knew this discussion was long overdue.

Janice hung up the phone. "At long last!" To herself. "God, give me strength!" For what exactly, she wasn't sure, but it never hurt to have Him on your side. Joline knew her Mom well, so she had strategically picked her Mom's favourite bistro to meet, right down to the exact table her Mom always sat at.

When Janice arrived, Joline and Erin were already seated. They both arose to give her a hug before settling in for a discussion long delayed. The maitre'd arrived as if on que, drinks in hand. "Mom, I knew what you'd like so I went ahead and ordered."

"Thanks baby. I'm so predictable, aren't I?"

"Mom."

"Yes?"

"There's something I need to tell you." Joline was really enjoying this.

Janice braced for what she knew was coming. She'd thought long and hard about this, even prayed about it. And she was determined not to overreact, under any circumstances.

"Mom, you know Erin and I've been friends for a couple of years now, right?" Janice nodded. "We've travelled together before, but only for a few days at a time. We weren't sure what the Camino would do to our friendship; six weeks on the road in less than ideal circumstances, would either break our friendship or bring us even closer together. I guess it's obvious which way that went." Joline paused before continuing on. "And when the bomb went off, and I thought I'd lost Erin forever, that's when I knew we'd be friends forever."

That's where Erin took over. "Joline's right. If there'd been any doubt in either of our minds, it was gone completely after that. I've always had a hard time getting close to anyone, but the way Joline stepped up and took care of me after that awful tragedy, convinced me that she really did love me, and that I really loved her."

Janice slowly began to nod her head. "I knew it. I've known it for a long time. Breath Janice, breath." All to herself.

Joline was watching Janice closely, trying to gauge her reaction to what Erin was saying.

"Mom, are you okay?"

"I'm fine, baby. Erin, please continue." Janice was doing her best to stay calm.

But Joline took over the reins. "Erin and I met in Chicago two summers ago. I was helping out at a makeshift soup kitchen at the time. We would take baskets of sandwiches to the park with us where we knew a lot of the homeless hung out. Someone usually had a guitar, and one of the guys would conduct a short service before we distributed the food. Oh, and they handed out other stuff as well: toothbrushes, soap, socks, shampoo, and so on. And on some occasions, even Bibles."

Erin butted in. "And that's where I met Joline. I was one of those homeless people. And the last person I wanted to talk to was some religious freak! So of course, who did I end up talking to? A religious freak! No, just kidding. She was with them though, and I kept an eye on her for a few days. She was always happy. I thought she must be a fake. No one's that happy. At least not me. I don't know if I'd ever been really happy in my life. Yet here she was. Even when people were mean to her. I didn't get it." Erin paused and Joline jumped back in.

"For days on end, every time I approached Erin to give her a sandwich or something, she just glared at me. So I decided to try something different. She was sitting on the ground below the tree she seemed to have claimed, so I offered her a sandwich, as usual. She took it, but instead of heading back to the group like I usually did, I plunked myself down beside her, and grabbed a sandwich for myself.

We ate in silence for a bit, but I noticed her glancing at me whenever I wasn't looking. So I started talking to her. If she decided to ignore me, I'd just keep talking."

"And that's what she did. She didn't stop, so finally, I had no choice. So I asked her why she always so happy. And she gave me this dumb answer, or at least that's what I thought at the time. "It's a choice. I choose to be happy." What a bunch of crap!" Erin chuckled. "But at least she was talking to me. No one talked to me the whole time I was there, unless they wanted something from me. She didn't want anything. Just to talk."

Joline took a turn. "I went back the next day, and Erin was still under the same tree. But this time, she actually greeted me. And she smiled. And I knew something had changed when she said "I can smile if I want to. It's my choice, you know!" And that's where our friendship really began!"

Janice loved the story but she still wasn't sure exactly what she was hearing. And she didn't want to ask. "Just listen, Janice. Don't say a word." To herself as usual.

Erin wanted to continue. "I'd been terribly abused as a child, and the first chance I got, I ran away. I ended up on the streets, got into the drug scene and everything that goes with that. I finally managed to crawl out of that hole but before long, I was in another. This time I was the one in a bad relationship. One night, I'd had to much to drink and decided to end the pain once and for all." That's when she showed

Janice her wrists. Janice winced and quickly glanced away. Joline felt for her Mom, but her Mom needed to hear this for herself.

"I woke up in the hospital. I was still alive! And that's when I began to think that maybe there really was a God. But, a few days later I was back on the streets, and as far as I could tell, He wasn't there. I was so lonely, and so afraid, and that's when Sam came along. Within a day we were in a relationship. Someone actually loved me! I was over the moon! Until I found out I was just one of a long line of lovers. And that's when I said to hell with it. From now on, it's just me. I don't need anybody!"

Joline spoke up. "But of course she did. And that's when I came along. It took awhile, but eventually she began to trust me, and the group. Next thing you know, she was passing out sandwiches to other homeless people. That's when we moved in together. I had an apartment close by, and Erin got a job at a bistro down the street."

"My turn to talk. For the first time in my life, I had a real job! I could pay my share of the rent, and I could buy some clothes. And even take Joline out for a drink. It was incredible!"

Joline jumped in again. "That's when I decided I needed to move on. I had a group I was supposed to meet up with a month earlier, but I wanted to make sure Erin was settled first. We hated to part, but I had my life and she was doing great now, and anxious to establish her own life. We had the lease switched over to her name and I joined my group in Scotland."

Janice was even more confused now. "So you left her? I thought you loved her. You don't just walk out of a relationship like that, do you?" Poor Janice.

Joline and Erin exchanged glances and then they began to giggle. Tears streamed down their faces but Janice was finding none of this very funny.

"And now you're here together. God, I'm confused!"

"Okay Mom, Erin and I do love each other . . . as friends. Best friends actually. I think at one point we weren't too sure where this was going, but we soon found out that that's exactly what we were. Friends."

Erin spoke next. "I love your daughter with all my heart, but I'm gay, and she's as straight as an arrow. That's probably why we're such good friends. Absolutely no expectations."

Janice sunk back into her chair, stunned. "I thought, I thought you were going to tell me you were gay. All this time I kept thinking, Joline's gay. How'll I tell your Grammy and Gramps? Oh my God, sorry Erin, I didn't mean anything by that. I don't care if you're gay or not. Oh my God!"

"Mom, if I was gay, I would've told you a long time ago, and I would've told Grammy and Gramps as well. You should've known that! I knew you'd still love me, regardless of anything, actually. Wouldn't you?"

"God, yes, of course I would! I'm exhausted!" Janice couldn't have faked it I'd she'd wanted to. "And Erin, I love you too. I don't care if you're gay or not! I shouldn't have said that. I going to stop talking now."

WE HAD NO CHOICE

DOUG AND GERALD LIVED in the same complex, attended the same school, and even dropped out around the same time. Even joined the same gang. And eventually they both graduated. From selling soft drugs to hard, from threatening people to assaulting them, from using knuckle busters to knives and guns.

And they graduated within the system as well. At first there were the warnings, then several stints in Juvie, followed by several overnighters in the local jail, and eventually longer term stays in the big house for everything from assault to attempted murder. And they had indeed committed murder, but so far they'd managed to escape the long arm of the law on those particular charges.

They wore their battle scars with pride. They worked as enforcers whenever they could, and as a result, they were respected on the street. And protected by their bosses. So whatever job came their way, they did, no questions asked.

That's when they met Mikey for the first time. It was nothing personal. Simply beat the hell out of him; threaten his girlfriend; make sure he got the message loud and clear; make it look real messy, and get the hell out of there. Nothing to it. They'd did this exact thing to countless others who had crossed the boss.

They cased the place the previous night, making sure of their escape route, and headed out for a few drinks as per usual. They arrived early the next evening, far enough away so as not to attract attention, and settled in for what could be a long wait.

Mikey and Janice arrived pretty much as they'd predicted. Now as long as he doesn't decide to stay, it's a go. If he stays, then we'll wait for another opportunity. But he didn't stay, and the boys did their job in fine fashion, professionals that they were. Then they took their leave. But what they didn't know was that Mikey had seen their tattoos, and that would come back to haunt them. Pretty damn soon.

Mikey knew he'd changed. He'd become a man of peace, a man of God, and yet now all he could think about was revenge. So what if they beat him up? No big deal! But, they killed Enrico to send me a message, and they threatened to kill Janice. And those are both unforgivable! At least by me!

Derek was no help. So he'd snooped a little when Derek was called out of his office the other day, and he just happened to see photos of the suspects, and their names. The police were looking into the matter. Arrests were imminent. "Not if I find them first!" Mikey wanted these guys bad.

It wasn't like Mikey didn't have connections. He had as many as he wanted, but he chose another path while in prison, and now served the Lord. But now he was a free man. He had a choice to make, but he knew he'd already made it.

So he tendered his resignation. Pastor Rick refused it. "Mikey, talk to me. Don't shut me out. You're a man of the cloth. You can't just quit." But of course he could. But finally he acquiesced. "Okay, I'll agree to a three month leave of absence. And then we'll see. I'm sorry, but there's something I have to do." And with that Mikey turned his back on the church. Hopefully, for a short time only. Pastor Rick watched him slowly walk away. "Please God, protect Mikey from himself."

Mikey knew that he'd already crossed the line, perhaps not yet in deed, but definitely in thought. So he made a couple of calls, knowing full well that this would indebt him to these same individuals in the future.

He thought of Janice and what this was doing to her. She couldn't understand why he'd pulled away from her. That was the hardest thing he'd ever done. He knew he loved her, and he was pretty sure she was beginning to feel the same. But after that threat on her life? All because of him? He'd rather lose her this way than see her lying dead somewhere. So he'd walked away. And when he caught them, they'd pay all right!

It didn't take long to spot them. They were exactly where the contact had said they'd be. Well, he'd become the watcher for awhile. Three nights later he decided to make his move. They always left the bar at the same time. It appeared that their only friend was each other. And they always followed the exact same route. And as usual, they were dead drunk. Good.

He'd have to take out the bigger one first. The lead pipe he'd acquired should do quite nicely, thank you very much. And here they come. Just a few more steps. "Hi guys. It's been awhile." They looked up, startled, but it wouldn't matter. It felt good, kinda like when the bat made contact with that other punks knee. But this was a head shot. Down he went. The other punk tried to run, but a shot to the shin brought him to the ground. Lead pipe: 2. Bad guys: 0. But Mikey didn't stop there. He'd prepared himself for this occasion, dressed for it, wore the appropriate gloves (the lead backed ones), and left them in the same state they'd left him. He wanted to finish the job. But he couldn't. So he made an anonymous call. To 911. He waited until he saw the cops arrive, and then faded into the night.

He expected the call the next morning. From Derek. "Just wanted you to know that the suspects in your beating case have been arrested. They're currently in the hospital. Apparently they ran into a lead pipe or something. I don't suppose you'd know anything about that?"

"No. Sorry. Why would I?" Mikey knew that Derek knew. But he wouldn't be hearing it from him.

O'Malley was relaxing in the lazy boy, sipping on his tea, but listening intently to Mikey's side of the conversation. "Don't mean to snoop but is everything alright?" Mikey had being acting strangely ever since the beating.

"Actually, its better than alright. Apparently they caught the punks that laid a beating on me."

O'Malley shook his head. But not at Mikey's dispassionate statement. Because he also had something to share with Mikey. And that would not go over well!

O'MALLEY GOES SAILING

O'MALLEY HAD BEEN DOING a lot of praying these past few days, not to delay the inevitable, but for peace with the decision he was about to make. And how best to tell Mikey. He loved Mikey like the son he never had, and he knew Mikey loved him as well. There would be no easy way to tell him that his time here was numbered in days, not weeks or months. The cancer was inoperable, and the pain was becoming intolerable. He knew how he wanted this to end, and if he waited any longer, it'd be out of his hands.

He'd already made funeral arrangements, and he'd made the visit to his lawyer to ensure a smooth transition from his estate to his sole beneficiary, Mikey. Everything else had been taken care of, and he'd already spoken with Pastor Rick. He would've liked to speak with Claire but that would've been too hard. But he had to speak with Mikey. Especially now. Mikey was heading the wrong way fast, and if it was the last thing he did on this earth, and it likely would be, he needed to tell Mikey exactly how he felt about him. And he had to ask Mikey for a couple of favours.

"Mikey, I need you to do the eulogy. I'm sorry to put that on you but it's either you, or no eulogy." O'Malley had rehearsed that line a thousand times already. "And I need you to do me proud, son. You're special. And one more thing, don't you dare let Janice get away!" He had to chuckle at that one.

He had finally cornered Mikey. And they had talked. And they'd cried. But when they were done, Mikey agreed to give it his best shot. He admitted to O'Malley that he had blown it big time recently. But O'Malley already knew that and he knew about the leave of absence as well.

"Son, it's time. I need your help."

Mikey knew what he meant. There was nothing more to say. They headed down to the boat shed, retrieved the Tom Cat, rigged it accordingly, attached a note to the mast, and readied it for its voyage.

They came together on that beach one last time. Tears flowed unabashedly. O'Malley headed out to sea. Mikey watched until the Tom Cat disappeared from view. Still he sat there. For several hours. And then he headed to the church.

THE EULOGY

WATCHING O'MALLEY SAIL away was the hardest thing Mikey had ever done. He knew he could've stopped him. Just like he knew he wouldn't stop him. It was O'Malley's time. What happened next would be up to him and God.

But he had made some promises to O'Malley, and by the grace of God, he would honour them.

When he made his way to the church that night, Pastor Rick was waiting for him. They spoke not a word. They went to the front of the church, both got down on their knees, and prayed to the God of the Universe, the God of Heaven and Earth. Each in their own way; each in their own time. And then Mikey went home.

Mikey stood tall and proud at the podium. And he cried as a real man would, unashamedly. He spoke of this incredible man that few really knew. And he spoke of this man who called him "son," and whom he called "father." And he spoke of the promises he had made to his earthly father, and of the promises he had made to his Heavenly Father. There would be no dry eyes that day.

He tried to avoid eye contact with Janice but it was inevitable that their eyes would meet. She wanted to rush to him, to hold him, to comfort this beautiful man. But she didn't. Later she would. "Mikey, I'm here. I'll always be here." She was shocked at her own words. But it was true and she knew it was.

O'Malley had made a choice. Mikey and Rick both knew of that choice. Both chose not to disclose it. O'Malley had gone sailing, as he often did, and something had obviously gone wrong. It was tragic but everyone knew he was happiest when he was out at sea. Claire wasn't buying it. O'Malley wouldn't make that kind of a mistake.

"Mikey, we have to talk. About O'Malley." Claire never got a lot of marks for sensitivity.

He knew there was no use in trying to con Claire. So he told her. "Happy now?"

JANICE AND MIKEY RECONNECT

CLAIRE THOUGHT MIKEY WAS being absolutely ridiculous cutting Janice loose like that. "Why didn't he just man up and tell her the truth, for God's sake? She can take it!" Claire was beside herself. "I'm telling her the truth. Men!" And that's what she did. Derek was annoyed at her, since he'd let the cat out of the bag during some pillow talk, and now she'd told Janice. "Women!"

So Janice knew. Obviously, the news shook her up. "For God's sake, Mikey, I'm a grown woman! Do you have any idea what I've gone through?" That's what she wanted to say. Instead, she'd stayed silent. But seeing him up on the podium pouring out his heart was more than she could take. He needed her, and damn it, she needed him!

"Hi Mikey."

He turned, their eyes locked, and without a single word being spoken, they melted into each other's arms. He started to sob. She held him even closer until he regained control. "Let's get out of here." He nodded and followed her to the door.

Mikey looked back, not sure if he should stay a bit longer, but Pastor Rick motioned him go. "I'll finish up. Get out of here." Just loud enough for Mikey to hear. Mikey nodded at him and followed Janice out to her vehicle. "Jump in. We'll pick yours up later."

He leaned back into the seat. These two didn't need to make small talk. She drove; he stared out the window, until she pulled into the drive thru. "Decent coffee, thank God!" He reached over and caressed her arm. Neither spoke.

Instead, they drove out to the boat house. Where O'Malley's boat still resided. Except now it was Mikey's. They were rather well dressed for the beach but that didn't really matter. They walked arm in arm down to the spot that O'Malley launched from. An hour later, as the sun began to set, they made their way back to Janice's car. They'd make one more stop to pick Mikey's vehicle up. Then he'd follow her home.

MIKEY COMES CLEAN

IKEY AND JANICE SPENT the entire night talking. About everything. He held nothing back, including his love for her. But if he had to sacrifice himself to save her, it would be worth it. Better for him to lose her love, than for her to lose her life. Everything was on the table. He talked. She listened. Then finally he stopped. She barely said two words the entire time. It would be her turn another day. She'd do the talking. He'd do the listening. But right now, they were both exhausted.

She walked him to the door. They embraced silently, and he took his leave. Janice watched as he got in his vehicle, and waited until he drove away before heading for bed. They'd talked all night. And now she was going to bed. Exhausted completely. But she knew if she entered the world of dreams these next few hours, they'd be very good ones!

Mikey slowly drove to O'Malley's place. He shook his head. "I guess it's my place now." But under his breath "It'll always be O'Malley's. God, I miss him." He too was beyond exhaustion, but strangely euphoric. He pulled into the driveway but before going into the house, he headed down to the boathouse. He needed to touch the Tom Cat. That's all, but he needed to do it. Then he, like Janice, settled down for what he hoped would be a long, dream filled sleep.

DEREK'S TAKE

WHEN CLAIRE INFORMED HIM that she needed to go to Houston for an important meeting, it didn't surprise him one bit. "Here we go again." Why they'd ever thought they could have a normal life was beyond him. Hell, they'd even went to an adoption agency! And Claire had changed dramatically, or so it seemed. She was embracing motherhood, and she'd began mentoring some of the apprentices at the paper. He actually had a wife!

And now, all hell had broken loose again. It's not like he blamed her for wanting to meet the threat head on; he'd have done the exact same thing. But, when she got her teeth into something, nothing else mattered. Not even him.

And Mikey. My friend. Claire's brother. And again Derek shook his head. "I'd do damn near anything for these guys, but they're gonna be the death of me yet." He loved talking to himself. And then he snickered " Actually, it almost was!" Of course there was no usable evidence. Obviously the cut lines were done deliberately, but unless some one came forward that had seen it happen, there was nothing else to go on. That's what pushed Claire over the edge. So here they were. He in Seattle, she, enroute to Houston.

" Mikey. I know you put those punks in the hospital. I know they deserved it, but you can't take the law into your own hands! Geez. And you're a Pastor to top it off! What the hell were you thinking?" Derek

31

was practically yelling at himself. And then. "Thank God you didn't leave any evidence!"

Derek was doing his best not to get ahead of himself. They were a family already, and they'd be a bigger family some day. When all this crap blew over! He refused to add "if" to that statement. They were going to have to face the fact that both of them were in careers that exposed them to the dregs of society, and that shoulder checks were always going to be part of their lives.

It was also becoming apparent that they both had some work to do on themselves, and as a couple, before they had children. Maybe not getting the children was a blessing in disguise. "Maybe we should start with a dog."

THE TIME HAS COME

CLAIRE WAS ON TIME. That's one thing she had learned about her boss. Don't ever be late! She headed for the boardroom as he'd instructed. He sat there alone. Strange. No customary greeting.

"Come in, Claire. Close the door." She'd never seen him like this.

She wanted to speak but thought that unwise. She bit her lip. "What the hell is going on?" To herself. She was beginning to get the picture, and she didn't like what she was seeing.

"Claire, you know why you're here."

"Yes, of course." Don't say anything else.

"We've had this conversation dozens of times over the years." It was true. "And I've bailed you out every time. But this last fiasco? I'm done, Claire. It's over." He paused and before she could speak, he added "You're fired. Your office has already been packed up. Everything will be sent to your home address. Your access codes have all been cancelled. This is not negotiable. I will personally walk you to the door." With that, he got up and headed towards the door.

"Wait a minute." Claire barely whispered the words. "Please."

He sighed, sat back down, and motioned for her to continue.

She proceeded cautiously. "I know that I screwed up. But, someone just tried to kill Derek. I thought if I could make him angry enough he might just say something that would incriminate him. I know I should have called you. I'm really sorry. I am. Please believe me." Claire was practically pleading by this time.

"Claire, you're always sorry after the fact. But this decision comes from far above my pay grade. And to be honest with you, I agree with this decision. I wish it didn't have to end this way, but it does. I'm sorry Claire. It's over." And with that, he got up once again, motioned her come, and escorted her to the street.

"Claire. I love you like a daughter. I always will. This is the hardest thing I've ever had to do, but either I do this, or I might as well pack my bags. I nearly did, but that still wouldn't have saved you. I hope one day we can have a proper conversation but that'll be up to you. I'm sorry. I have to go." He left her standing there staring at his re-treating figure until he disappeared in the folds of the waiting elevator.

There was nothing to say. She slowly made her way to the bistro down the street. The one she and her boss used to slip to whenever they wanted to have a chat "off the record." Except now she was alone. And her task had just become decidedly more complicated.

But anyone knowing Claire would know that this sudden turn of fortune would make her all the more determined to find that bastard. She still had connections, and now she wouldn't have to stay within the paper's guidelines. She decided to head a bit further down the street to the establishment that served up something a little more po-tent than coffee.

How the hell was she going to explain this to Derek? As if he'd be surprised anyway. And that this would put her at even greater risk since now she'd be completely on her own. Oh, and by the way, I guess you're the sole supporter in our household now. Claire was not look-ing forward to this one bit!

"Maybe I won't tell him just yet. I do have some savings, and I know I'll get a decent payout. It's not like he knows much about my work anyway." Claire was already working out the details in her mind. "As far as he knows I'm doing what I always do. Yeah, that should work."

JANICE REBOOTED

J ANICE SAT AT HER WRITING table, notepad at the ready, pen in hand, attempting to make sense of this life she called her own. Surreal came to mind but even that was inadequate. Finally, she began to jot down random thoughts. Some would call it brain storming, others would refer to it as mind mapping. She simply called it difficult. "Come on Janice, you've done this a thousand times." To herself. So she began jotting down random words: Jason, writer, serial killer, Mikey, Tom Cat, love, betrayal, Joline, Erin, best seller, mom and Dad, God, prison, and a hundred more.

She set aside her pen, studied the list, and then set it aside. She knew she was going somewhere with this but she was having trouble deciding where. She'd always written children's stories based around Joline. Then she'd started a series about twins and their incredibly complicated lives, and for a time she'd considered writing about, of all things, a serial killer. That had never really gone anywhere but she knew she needed to begin writing again. Her audience was calling for some new releases, unfortunately, writing about children or the teen twins dilemmas left her completely cold.

"Am I a writer or not? Come on girl, get your act together." She was great at this self talk. The sad part was that she already knew the answer, at least part of it. She was done with the previous writing. It had been very good to her, even made her a great living, but her gut told her it was time to write about "real life" from here on in. And she'd certainly been involved in a whole lot of that this past while.

And then it struck her. "I know! I'll write about my own life, warts and all. Thank about it?" Now she was beginning to get excited. "Let's see. I married a serial killer. My family was threatened if I didn't find a notebook that Jason had stolen. My adopted sister came back into my life after abandoning us as a family. And her husband is a homicide detective. Someone just tried to kill him. Plus, Mikey was shot but he wasn't the target. And I'm in love with Mikey who just so happens to be a Pastor, who was put in jail when he was fifteen years for killing his dad to save his sister, Claire, which is the girl my parents adopted. Oh my God! This is crazy" she was on a roll now.

If there wasn't a book somewhere in this mess of a life, then she wasn't the writer everyone claimed she was. "This is getting exciting!" But she'd keep all of this to herself. At least for now. "This is perfect!"

MIKEY'S HONOUR

O'MALLEY'S DECISION TO GO sailing one final time would stay with Mikey forever. To sail off into the sunset knowing it would be a one way trip had to have taken a tremendous amount of courage. But O'Malley would live on through Mikey's promises; promises not made only to him but to God himself. He'd treated Mikey like a son. He'd did his best to offer advice, course correct whenever possible, but still allow this young man the freedom to make his own choices. Coming out of the big house after a thirty year stint and expecting to have a normal life was really expecting too much, and yet Mikey had done pretty damn well.

When Mikey got involved with the prison reform from the outside, and all hell had broken loose, it would've been a lot easier for him if he'd gone along with the status quo and looked the other way. He didn't do that, and he'd paid dearly as a result, plus Enrico had been murdered. That's when Mikey nearly went over to the other side. He was a Pastor; a pastor that preached love, but now the only thing he wanted was revenge.

O'Malley saw this, and although he knew Mikey was walking on the other side of the line, he'd do his best to pull him back to safety. When he got his diagnosis, he knew what he had to do. If that's what it took to bring Mikey back home, than by God, that's what he'd do.

And it worked. Mikey was a man of honour, and now he'd given his word. O'Malley had always loved sailing. He'd dreamed about sailing around the world, and though this might not quite be the same thing, he'd have the great honour of sailing from this world into the next.

MIKEY GOES TO CHURCH

IKEY MADE HIS WAY BACK to the church a day after the funeral. And as usual, Pastor Rick was waiting for him. The moment Mikey walked through the door, Rick knew that he really was back, and now they could get down to business. This was a lost world and there was much to do. It was time to leave the drama of their everyday lives in their proper place and help those most in need, wherever they may be, and many of them were right here among us.

CLAIRE'S JOURNEY

C LAIRE DECIDED THAT SHE'D be wise to get on board with the rival paper that had been trying to hire her for years. It made sense financially, and it would certainly show her paper a thing or two! Besides, that way she wouldn't have to lie to Derek.

But first, she had a little digging to do that perhaps skirted the "rules" a wee bit. Best to get those done before she committed herself to anyone else. Just in case. So she made a call. Not to someone she particularly liked but someone in the know. Someone who could get the info she needed. For a price, of course.

Within a day she had the info she needed. She may well need another bath after that meeting, but when the scumbag got up close and personal with her, and then Derek, he'd crossed a line of no return. He'd pay dearly for what he'd done to them. And now she'd lost her job, and it was his fault!

Her investigative reporting had taken her all over the country so it wasn't unusual for her to be in different cities from time to time. At first Derek found that hard to understand. So when she called him from Atlanta or New York he'd always be taken aback at first. Most people expected their spouse to come home each evening; he didn't know if she was even in the same state! But that certainly made it easier for her to explain her absences, and since this one was off the books, she saw no need to tell him about her current lack of a job just yet.

This would take some finesse to pull off. Her perpetrator was obviously in Seattle, or so it seemed, so she'd have to be in Seattle as well. Home. With Derek. Bummer. She felt guilty the moment she thought that, but it would be a lot easier to pull it off if it was happening somewhere else.

"Hi hon." Claire decided it would be wise to stop by Derek's office for a bit.

"Hey. Hi babe, I wasn't expecting you back so soon. Everything ok?"

"Everything's great. I decided that I might as well work from home. Most of my work is on the computer right now anyway, so I might as well be home as much as possible. Never know when I might have to take off again. Missed you!"

"Sorry hon. I'm not ignoring you but I'm right in the middle of something. Maybe we could meet for lunch?" Derek was trying not to be dismissive but . . .

So they more or less settled back into their lives. There'd been the two incidences but nothing since. Perhaps it was over but Claire had her doubts. And then she got the call. The voice was obviously disguised but the message was clear enough. "I'm coming for you. Maybe today, next week, next month. I have lots of time. Enjoy the time you have, and say good bye to your loved ones!" And that was that. She stared at the phone knowing full well that this was no joke. Either she took him out or he'd take her out. And she wasn't even sure who she was dealing with. Not yet.

BON VOYAGE

I T WAS TIME. ERIN WAS settling in; the physical injuries were a thing of the past and the bistro was attracting a steady flow of customers. Perfect! Now Joline could leave in good conscience. She'd already said her goodbyes to her mom and grandparents, and the rest of the gang. She'd held off going an extra month to ensure that Erin was indeed ready to fly on her own.

The Smithsonian Tropical Research Institute-Bocas Del Toro, in Panama had accepted her as one of several international students to work at the facility for a semester. Her semester at sea had paid off big time and now she was going to Panama! She had wanted to go a few weeks earlier to explore the country before she started her semester but she would make that up after her tour of duty. No big deal.

Twelve hours later she arrived in Panama City, tired but excited. She only had a couple of days before she had to check in at the Institute so she decided to sightsee as much as she could before heading to the island. Even the trip from Tocumen International Airport proved interesting. Beautiful views, and then she had to laugh, for off to her right stood the Trump Ocean Club Hotel. "My God, he's everywhere!" Joline shook her head. "Too rich for my blood."

So she settled in for the night and next morning she went exploring. She marvelled at the incredible architecture of the high rises of the financial district. And she shook her head in awe at Panama City's

Diablo Rojo (Red Devils) buses (converted Bluebird school buses), as they cruised the streets with lights flashing and music blaring, raging colour schemes, and straight pipes attached. Don't get on them. Much safer to just watch from a distance as they raced each other down the street, passengers hanging outside the door, as they one upped the other buses. She was even surprised to see them as most of them were now in a bus graveyard, and soon these would follow. Such is life.

After exploring the downtown, she headed for the old city. She'd been advised to do this during the day, never in the evening, and hide your jewellery, please. This walking adventure took her through the side streets of China town and ultimately to the old town, the area known as Casco Viejo where the presidential palace still exists.

And then the guide waved Joline over. "Quick, señorita. Listen." She heard an approaching helicopter. "What am I looking for?"

"El Presidente!"

Sure enough. It was. "That's Juan Carlos Varela, right?"

"Si."

She'd studied Panama's history before she'd left home, but this topped the cake! She'd have some stories to tell after this trip. "I need to get blogging as soon as I get back to the room."

"One more day before I head to Bocas Del Toro. I need to go to the canal." Talking to herself as usual. She made the arrangements and the next morning she was at the locks of Miraflores where she'd go through a couple of the locks aboard one of the tour boats that operated out of there.

And finally she was aboard, and overwhelmed. They were in a dinky little boat right next to a container ship that was at least 100 feet wide, and according to their guide, approximately 1000 feet long. Kinda scary. But finally it was their turn. That's when she found out that the boat she was on was formerly owned by no other than the infamous Al Capone. The Isla Morada had been significantly upgraded over its 100 year reign, and is no longer a rum runner, but it's well known in these parts. "How cool is that?" thought Joline. "Man, am I ever glad I ended up on this boat." She had to chuckle at herself. "I thought I ended up on the runt of the litter. I can't wait to blog about this!"

And that would take care of this day. Tomorrow morning she would be off to Bocas Del Toro. Panama for sure, but with a very different vibe than the big city.

MIKEY HAS A PROPOSAL

"**D**EREK, CAN WE MEET?" Mikey needed to pass his idea past Derek before he talked to anyone else.

"You bet. How about lunch if you're free?" Good. Derek wanted to have a chat with Mikey as well. He'd crossed a line and that didn't sit well with Derek. He'd bit his tongue at the time, but Mikey and Claire were obviously cut from the same cloth, and it was time to clear the air.

"Ok, Mikey, keep your cool. You screwed up. You know it. Derek knows it. Whatever he throws at you, take it. Suck it up. Got it?" Mikey loved to talk to himself. Hopefully he'd get his own message.

Derek was talking to himself as well. "Ok Derek, Mikey knows he screwed up. He's coming to you. Listen to what he has to say before you say a word. Got it?"

And that's how they would meet. A whole bunch of self talk should serve as the appetizers, and now both should be ready for the main course. Two reasonably intelligent men looking for a way to keep their fragile egos intact and still come out feeling like winners.

These two liked each other so that was definitely a bonus. They shook hands, made some small talk, and then Mikey got to it. He started by apologizing for his actions.

Derek nodded and Mikey went on. "Derek, I've been thinking a lot lately about whether I was really cut out for the ministry or not. My actions certainly said No Way, on that particular night. But I've spent a lot of time in prayer and I've spent time with Rick. He's my rock and he feels that I have far too much to offer to give up now. Derek, I need your honest opinion. I wouldn't ask it I didn't respect you so much, but I do. And by the way, this has nothing to do with Claire. I'm not talking to her about this. I love her but . . . I think you know what I mean."

Indeed he did.

Mikey began. "Those guys deserved what they got and a whole lot more but that doesn't excuse my actions. You'd told me to leave it to you but I was hell bent on revenge. It even surprised me but when they threatened Janice, I lost it. I even scared me. My God, I could have killed them! Then what? Fortunately that didn't happen. I understand that their court date is just a few days away and they'll likely get a couple of years in the slammer. But I want to propose something and I need your opinion." Mikey stopped to catch his breath so Derek took over.

"When it comes to the courts nothing is ever certain. The judge could throw the book at them or give them a suspended sentence. It's a crap shoot. Can I assume that you have a better idea?" Derek knew he did or he wouldn't be here right now.

"I do. I've talked at length to Pastor Rick about this, but I value your input, and you're not the bleeding heart that I am. You're a voice of reason and logic so here goes." Mikey took a deep breathe and continued on. "I want to work with these two guys for a few months. If the courts would allow it, I'd like to set up weekly counselling sessions instead of prison time. I think I can turn these guys around. Derek, I know these people. I've been around them for over 30 years. I think these guys can still be saved."

"Yep, you are a bleeding heart, no doubt about it. Do I agree with you? Actually, I do. If you're right, and you're able to turn them, I may not have to deal with them again, and then everyone wins. Do you realize that this doesn't even have to end up in the judge's hands? If we can get the lawyers to agree to a plea bargain, the judge would probably just rubber stamp it. But then it's on you. Are you sure you want that?"

"I do. And I know that it's about my own redemption as well, but Derek, I can do this!" Mikey was adamant. "Will you help me set this up? I m not even sure where to start."

If there was a way to keep criminals off the street, Derek was all in. Unfortunately most of these interventions didn't work all that well, but with Mikey feeling so guilty, there just might be a chance. Definitely worth a shot. "I'll help you. Come to the station Monday around 9 am and we'll get the ball rolling. Anything else?"

Mikey wasn't expecting it to be that easy. Of course it wasn't a done deal but now he had Derek on his side. "Thank you God!" Under his breath. "Thank you Derek. I really appreciate it. I'll do you proud, you just wait and see!"

And that's where they left that conversation. "Mikey, I have something to ask you now. Are you free for the rest of the day?"

"I could be. Why?"

"I want you to take me sailing on O'Malley's boat. Just for an hour or so."

Mikey could feel the blood draining from his face. "Uh yeah, I guess so." Crap! He was shocked at his own reaction. To himself. "A bit sensitive are we?"

Derek was studying Mikey carefully. "Listen, Mikey, we don't have to. Maybe another time. I'm sorry, I shouldn't have brought that up."

"No, that's fine. Yes. Let's do it. It just caught me by surprise, that's all. I haven't touched the Tom Cat since . . ."

"You're sure? Another day is fine. Seriously." Derek was kicking himself for bringing it up.

"Let's go!" And with that, Mikey waved the hostess over, paid the bill, and they headed down to the marina. Mikey would think about this later that night. Even he was surprised by his reaction. There were obviously a few issues he still needed to deal with as well. Perhaps grieving couldn't be put in a box all that easily.

O'Malley had taught Mikey how to sail. A better teacher he could not have asked for. Derek was impressed. Man, this little rig was fast, and Mikey knew exactly what he was doing. And that's how these two would go on to build an incredible friendship that would sustain them in the years ahead.

ON THE TRAIL

CLAIRE WAS PISSED. If this jerk thought he could intimate her, he obviously had no clue who he was dealing with! "I'll bury you!" The pit bull was definitely back. By this time she had her contacts working around the clock. Several names emerged but were soon eliminated. "My God, I didn't put that many away, did I?" But of course, she had. Not alone, mind you, but she'd be the one to break the story and to put it out there for the whole world to see. As a result, she became the face they most identified with. And now one of them wanted her dead. But in his own sweet time.

"What an idiot! If it were me, and I wanted someone gone, they'd never know what hit them. In and out. Over and done with." But thankfully for Claire, he didn't follow her advice, and as a result, she had time. How much, unknown, but more than she'd have given anyone. But she needed answers and sooner or later one of her associates would come through.

STRANGERS IN OUR HOME

D EREK FOUND HIMSELF staring at Claire from across the room. She was on the computer as usual, he flicking channels. Same room, thousands of miles apart. He was surprised at how little he cared. Just months before, they were going to start a family. Now he wasn't even sure who that other person in their house was.

He knew she was pretending to be interested in them. The only thing that mattered to Claire was breaking the case. Of course it was important, obviously, but this wouldn't end it. She'd find another case. And then another. This was her life. He shook his head. "Whatever." Under his breath.

And that's when Derek seriously began exploring his options. If they didn't "make it," then what? He shook his head even as he thought these words. "I never even considered this possibility. I must've been blind." Still, if their marriage fell apart . . .

Guaranteed, he'd stay in the homicide division. The few years with the cold case division pointed out to him just how much he loved homicide, not homicides of course, but the division. Plus, he was good at it. In fact, he may just decide to do some undercover work, certainly more dangerous but the rewards were damn near immeasurable. He could feel himself getting excited as his thoughts raced ahead to some imaginary scenario waiting for his arrival on the scene. "That'll show you!" Crap, he'd said that out loud.

"What'd you say, hon? Sorry, I missed it. My head was somewhere else."

That was close. Derek responded to Claire. "It was nothing. I was just thinking out loud. Sorry."

Claire came over to where Derek was sitting. She lowered herself into his lap, snuggled in and kissed him on the cheek. "I'm sorry I've been so distant lately." That's all it took for Derek to start second guessing himself. "Maybe it's just me. I've got to relax more. She's been through so much crap lately." All to himself of course. He should've added "And you've put me through a pile of crap ever since I've known you," but of course he didn't say that. He didn't say anything.

They spent the rest of the evening the way any loving couple should, and soon all of Derek's previous thoughts had taken flight once again. But as the sun slowly peaked into their bedroom the next morning he found himself analyzing her as she lay there. Perhaps this was the fantasy, not the other. He slipped from the bed silently, quickly showered, dressed, made a quick coffee, and headed for the door.

Claire had heard him shower, then she'd drifted back to sleep, but the smell of the coffee awakened her in time to hear Derek leaving. "Hon. Wait a minute." She ran to him, gave him a big kiss, and then informed him that she'd be out of town for a couple of days. "Sorry, I meant to tell you earlier. I'm so forgetful these days! Love you. I'll call. Bye."

Derek stepped through the doorway onto the front step, looked back at the closing door and shook his head. "Big surprise." He muttered to himself as he headed to his car.

AND AWAY SHE GOES . . . AGAIN

CLAIRE HAD JUST LIED TO Derek. She had no appointments. Even she was surprised at herself. "But I'm not sure about us. Damn! I thought I could be the perfect little housewife. What a joke!" Out loud to a very empty house. "I can't live like this!"

She'd never meant to deceive Derek. Never! She was sure she loved him, but now she wasn't even sure if she knew what love was. After all, she'd abandoned her family, hadn't she? Hadn't even bothered her that much, at least not at the time. And now she felt exactly the same as then. Trapped. And she didn't like it one bit! Her thoughts frightened her. "I'm so sorry Derek. I didn't mean for this to happen." Oh my God, had she actually said those words. Then she packed her suitcase, set the security system, and left. To where? Who knows. She didn't.

But then she got a call. "I can be there by this evening. Ok, bye." Now she had a destination. Perhaps she hadn't lied to Derek after all. One of her contacts had come through for her. He was in Portland, just a three hour drive from here. Perfect. Nothing like a road trip to get the juices flowing again. He said he had exactly what she was looking for, and bring cash. A quick stop at the ATM and she was on her way.

It was around 1 pm when she arrived. Time for a quick lunch and then a meeting with her contact. She always enjoyed Portland, especially down along the harbour. Besides, it was as good a place as any for a meeting.

"Beautiful day, hey?"

She glanced up. "You're early."

"So are you. You got something for me?"

Claire opened her purse just enough to convince him to part with the Manila envelope he carried under his arm. He handed it to her. She scanned its contents, nodded approvingly and handed him the envelope. A quick check and he was on his way.

"It's been a pleasure doing business with you." Then he was gone.

Claire could barely contain herself. This was the one. She knew it the moment she opened the file but dared not let her contact see her excitement. This is a money game. You'd better know how to play poker or expect to pay through the nose. Now she could go to work. It should have been obvious to her that the stalker was either from Seattle, the surrounding area, or at least within driving distance, but she'd put so many in the big house that she felt the threat could've come from anywhere. All they'd have to do is hire a hitman and that could be done from anywhere. But this made the most sense.

Now she had a name and his file. The hunter would now become the hunted. She'd enjoy this. And if she had to colour outside the lines, so be it. At least she didn't have an editor to answer to. And when she broke the story, it would be to the highest bidder. "How dare you throw me to the curb after everything I've done for you!"

His name was Richard Freshman. An incredible salesman, well respected in his industry, that is, until he sucked a whole raft of investors into a Ponzi scheme that totalled in the tens of millions of dollars. But an anonymous call to Claire put her on his trail, and after months of investigation, the Feds swooped in and arrested him. He didn't see it coming. Evidence was everywhere. He knew no bounds, and as a result, family, friends, and business associates were the main victims. Entire life savings were gone in a flash. But she'd hooked him and now he was headed for the big house.

Ironically, that's not what Claire was investigating. She knew him as a flesh peddler; his specialty, young boys. But either way, he was going down. He lost everything, family included. Now he was out. She was his target. And it had nothing to do with the Ponzi scheme.

Except now, he was hers. "How dare you threaten me!"

ERIN AND JANICE AND JOLINE

J ANICE WAS REALLY MISSING Joline. And she hadn't heard from her for a couple of weeks, which was unlike Joline. Maybe Erin had heard something. So Janice headed to the bistro. "Time for a break anyway." She thought to herself. Besides, she and Erin had become quite close over the past several months. She had become a surrogate Mom in a fashion, a role she very quickly accepted.

Erin saw her coming from down the street and when Janice stepped into the bistro she was greeted first by an all consuming hug from Erin followed by a cup of Janice's favourite coffee. "Hi Mom."

"Hi baby. You look great. I love seeing you so happy." Janice truly loved this girl. "What's going on? Tell me. You're holding out on me. I know you."

So Erin did. "Mom, I've met someone. I never thought I could feel this way about anyone, but Mom, she's the one! I'm dying to have you meet her!"

Janice was excited for Erin, definitely, but she was still getting used to being so open minded. It wasn't that she had any major hangup on the issue but it was the first time she'd ever actually dealt with someone who was openly gay. She had to chuckle at her own naivety. "How about if I invite the two of you over for dinner one evening? Would that work for you?"

"Oh my God, yes!" Erin jumped up and embraced Janice yet again. "I love you so much!" And then Erin asked the question on both their minds. "Have you heard from Joline?"

"No. I thought maybe you had. That's weird. She's always stayed in close contact. Maybe she's just busy."

"Let's call her right now." No answer. And no way to leave a message. Weird. "I'm sure she's fine. She'll call as soon as she can. She knows we're a couple of worry warts!" Erin shrugged as she hung up the phone.

And of course Joline did call. Two days later. "Sorry Mom, I knew you'd be freaking out but we were out at sea and there was no way I could call you. The voyage took a week longer than I'd expected. Sorry."

"I wasn't freaking out, I was just wondering why you hadn't called. Ok, maybe I was a little freaked out. But here you are! Are you enjoying yourself down there?"

"I love it, Mom! It's so interesting. I'm thinking about staying an extra semester if they'll let me. You've gotta come visit me if I stay here longer. How's Erin? I have to call her tonight for sure. She's probably freaking out as much as you are. Just kidding." Joline was on her game today. "And Granny and Gramps."

It was pretty clear to Janice that Joline was loving every minute of her time in Bocas. She missed her terribly but it was obvious that Joline was on top of the world. Good for her. You go, girl! And yes, she would definitely go visit her.

And then Joline called Erin. What a call; they filled each other in on everything. Erin's love life took centre stage of course, and Joline casually dropped a hint that she just might be seeing someone as well. "Don't you dare tell Mom!"

"Come on. Tell me everything. What's his name? Is it serious? Tell me!" Erin was beside herself.

"Nope. I'm not telling you anything else. When I have more to tell you, I'll tell you. Simple as that."

"Fine! Have it your way."

"Trust me. I will." Joline loved bugging Erin, and truthfully, Erin loved every minute of it. "And don't you dare tell Mom! Gotta go, someone's waiting. Bye." Erin could only stare at her phone but then she did a little happy dance right there in the bistro. "Yes!"

TAKE IT TO THE JUDGE

With Derek's help, Mikey built his case. He had Pastor Rick on board and of course, Derek. Doug and Gerald's lawyer was more than willing to go along if it would keep them out of jail.

Doug and Gerald weren't quite as eager when they were first offered the deal. "You want us to be alone with Mikey? He damn near killed us. How do you know he's not going to finish the job? I don't like this one bit." Gerald was anything but enthusiastic. Doug, on the other hand was all in. "As long as I don't gotta go to jail." One down. That's all it took. "I'm not taking the rap for the both of us. Fine. We just have to be good boys for six months, right?" Right.

And then the day arrived. The lawyers for the defence and the prosecution presented their case before the judge, and their bargain plea arrangement. There wasn't much for the judge to disagree with. They'd obviously done their homework. Great. "Ok boys, you're getting off easy. Don't let me see you in my court room again. Got it?"

"Yes sir."

"Yes sir."

And that was that. Now they had to go with Mikey. They weren't expecting it, and weren't quite sure how to handle it when Mikey came up to them, shook their hands, and then gave each of them a hug. He had to chuckle to himself as they both turned as red as beets when he embraced them.

They exchanged glances, wondering what they'd got themselves into. If they only knew. But Mikey knew, and he was determined to turn these guys around. Time would tell.

And that's when Derek and Rick knew for certain that Mikey was back!

Doug and Gerald didn't know what hit them. And now Mikey was loving them up instead of beating them with a lead pipe. "This guys nuts! He's trying to get us all religious. Watch him, Doug, I'm telling you."

Mikey decided that the best policy would be to see them separately. They were two peas in a pod, and maybe once he had one or the other on board, he could relax a little. Gerald appeared to be the alpha of the two. And that's who Mikey would concentrate on. "You're mine. You just don't know it yet!" Mikey rubbed his hands together in anticipation.

YOU FIRST, GERALD

S O MIKEY GOT HIS WISH. Arrangements had been made to board the two of them at a halfway house for the next six months. Each would have their own room and each would be accountable for their own actions. The twins were being separated whether they liked it or not. Now Mikey could get to work. He'd convinced the courts to let him work with them on a one on one basis for up to two hours per day, 3 days per week for the next six months. It was a huge commitment on Mikey's part but he had all the backing he needed. "Thank you Pastor Rick, and thank you God."

He set up their schedules, ensured there was no misunderstanding, and set the wheels in motion. That's when he called Gerald to meet him the next morning at the church.

"Why the church?" Gerald wasn't giving up control easily. No one could push him around.

"Why not?"

Gerald shrugged. "Fine." The next morning, promptly at 9, Mikey found him sitting on the bench next to the church awaiting his arrival.

"Morning Gerald."

Gerald said nothing. Just stared at Mikey. Inwardly Mikey smiled to himself. They were two alphas tangling in the jungle and there could only be one victor. And it wouldn't be Gerald. He just didn't know that yet.

"Let's go for a walk." Mikey motioned for Gerald to come. Once again, he shrugged but joined a Mikey on his self styled journey to redemption. The next hour and a half was forced small talk but Gerald was obviously beginning to relax, at least a little. My God, he even laughed a couple of times before he remembered that that was totally uncool. And finally it was over. "See you Wednesday at 9. Enjoy the rest of your day. And with that, Mikey turned around and headed the other way, leaving Gerald somewhat confused. "If that's all I have to do to keep him happy this'll be a breeze!" Then he headed back to the halfway house.

Doug was waiting for him. "How'd it go? Come on. I wanna know everything. I gotta see him this afternoon."

"It went good. All we did was walk and talk. Well, he did most of the talking."

"That's it? You just talked? What the hell? Are you lying to me?" Doug was confused.

He shouldn't have said that. Gerald smacked him across the side of the head, then grabbed him by the collar. "Don't ever call me a liar. Ever!" And with that he left Doug standing there nursing his jaw and wondering what the hell just happened.

And then it was Doug's turn. But this time Mikey would come to him. "Jump in Doug. We're going for a ride."

"Crap." To himself. "Where the hell's he taking me? I don't like this one bit!" It's amazing how tough these punks can be in their own environment and so totally insecure when their control is taken away.

Barely a word was spoken between the two men as they made their way to their destination. But what Doug didn't know was that Mikey had uncovered some information on him that just might prove useful. He'd know if he was right soon enough.

"We're here. Come on, I have someone I want you to meet." Doug reluctantly followed him into the building before realizing where he was.

"Is this an animal shelter?" Doug was starting to get excited.

"It is. Doug, I'd like you to meet Carla. She runs the place."

"Hi Doug, great to meet you."

"Yeah, hi." No one ever liked to meet Doug. What the hell?

Carla and Mikey had discussed this well in advance but Doug didn't need to know that. "Doug, why don't you take a look around. Mikey and I need to discuss some business. It'll just take a few minutes. Is this ok?"

"Yeah, ok." And with that Doug made his way into the shelter. And that's when the two of them settled back into Clara's office and watched the cameras slowly peel back the layers of onion. Soon Doug's smiles became giggles as he held one precious animal after another. He cuddled them, they cuddled him. Mikey and Carla high fived. Mikey had played a hunch. And now he had a way to reach Doug. Yes!

"Hey Doug, we gotta go."

"Already?"

The oh so silent trip to the shelter was anything but on the way back to the house. Mikey didn't have to say a word. In fact, he couldn't have if he wanted to. Doug wouldn't shut up! "Can we go back on Wednesday?"

"You bet. See you then." Day one was done. Not bad, Mikey, not bad at all.

TABLE FOR 4 PLEASE

TONIGHT WAS THE NIGHT. Janice booked their favourite table at their favourite restaurant. At first she'd thought about just inviting Erin and her date but decided she wanted Mikey there with her. Less awkward. Actually, she didn't really know what she thought. "Relax, Janice, for God's sake. Relax."

She'd prepped Mikey on the particulars of this evening ahead of time. He just shrugged his shoulders. "Why don't we just go and enjoy ourselves? Let's see where it goes. It's no big deal."

Of course he was right. I mean, they were just going out to eat and enjoy each other's company, right? Right. Janice shook her head. Why did she have to always make such a big deal out of everything? I wonder if Joline knows about this? Of course she does. She and Erin are best friends, remember. She's probably waiting for Erin's call right after dinner to tell her how I handled the dinner. I betcha!" Now she was in a tizzy. "Janice, smarten up!"

Mikey and Janice arrived first, secured their table, order a glass of wine and settled in for what should prove to be a very interesting evening. Less than ten minutes later Mikey nudged Janice. "They're here."

Janice could tell that Erin was every bit as nervous as she, so she promptly stood up and stepped forward to give Erin one of her famous bear hugs, and then introduced herself to Erin's date. I'm Janice, I'm so pleased to meet you. And this is Mikey."

"Erin's told me so much about you. I'm Sylvia." She reached out and embraced Janice warmly, and then extended her hand to Mikey. "Hi Mikey."

It appeared that all that worry had been a colossal waste of time. But now it was time for a drink. And several hours of spirited conversation.

"My God! Look at the time. I'm sorry to bust up the party but I've got an early morning meeting. Sorry!" Sylvia was sure her watch must've skipped ahead a couple of hours. "I had a wonderful time. Thanks so much for inviting me."

Hugs all around and then Erin and Sylvia were on their way. Mikey and Janice decided they needed one more glass of wine to finish off what had been a perfect evening. And besides, cab drivers needed to make a living too. Mikey's vehicle would be quite fine parked where it was until morning.

CLAIRE MAKES HER MOVE

NOW SHE WAS IN CHARGE. And he didn't even know she was in town. Perfect. Within a couple of days she knew his routine right down to when he left the house in the morning and when he shut off his bedroom light at night. She knew who he visited, who his business associates were, and who his lover was.

She'd arranged to have his house bugged as well as his vehicle tagged. He may have thought he was good at the stalking game but she was a master at it. How she'd love to take him down with some good old fashioned justice! But, she'd build her case instead, and put him back in a cell to rot. He'd crossed a line of no return when he'd threatened her family. Threaten me, fine. My family? You're done!

Claire decided she'd better head home for a few days to keep Derek pacified. A little sucking up is all it'd take, but truthfully, she'd rather not go home at all. She shook her head at her own thoughts. "I'm going to have to deal with this sooner or later. I love this life! Even if I'm alone most of the time."

Everything Richard said was being recorded, and forwarded to her automatically. She'd even know if he decided to pay her a visit. Her hand instinctively reached for her purse. She'd never had to use the 45 before, but she'd always kept it close by. Derek didn't even know she had it. Why bother freaking him out. Besides, it was illegal. And she spent plenty of time at the range. He didn't know that either.

She'd received several offers from competing papers since her unceremonious dumping by her boss. Perhaps now was the time to have a chat with a couple of them. She knew she was in control, and as long as they'd let her work on cases of her choice, she was prepared to sign a long term contract. She would even be prepared to move if that was deemed necessary. Yep, she and Derek had better have the talk real soon. Well, after she'd signed a contract, of course.

Claire loved her family, and Derek. But it wasn't enough. And it was impossible to make them understand where she was coming from when she didn't even know herself. Still, she'd better go visit the gang this weekend before all hell broke loose. It was going to happen. Sooner or later.

DEREK READIES FOR THE STORM

CLAIRE HADN'T CALLED LIKE she'd promised to. As usual. It used to bother Derek immensely. There's got to be something wrong; maybe she's hurt and can't call, or she'd had an accident, something. Surely she'd call if she could. But he'd learned a long time ago that none of the above were necessary for her not to call. It was just Claire. Oh, she'd always apologize after she was called on it.

"I'm so sorry. I meant to and then I got busy, and . . . please forgive me. I promise not to do it again. Love you." And of course she always got away with it.

But he'd grown tired of her excuses. Anytime now she'd burst through the door, throw her arms around him, mumble an apology, and go on as if nothing had ever happened. "One of these days, she'd burst through that door expecting her dutiful husband to be waiting, and I won't be here. Don't push me Claire. I've had it up to here!" Derek was great at talking the talk to himself. "Derek, you gotta talk to her. This is a bunch of crap!"

And then, as if on que, Claire did indeed burst through the door, rush over to Derek, give him an extra long kiss, mumble her apology, and headed for the bedroom. "These shoes are killing me. Why don't you pour us a glass of wine, hon? I'll just be a moment. Love you."

Derek sighed, but as usual, did as he was instructed. "I can't believe that this is my life. I loved you so much Claire." He shook his head, dimmed the lights, and settled into another artificial evening with the "love" of his life. "Thank God the adoption had fallen through!"

SECOND TIMES A CHARM

IKEY DECIDED TO MEET Gerald down on the boardwalk once again. When he arrived, Gerald was already there, looking bored as usual. They exchanged pleasantries, well, at least Mikey did. Gerald just grunted. "Let's go."

Neither spoke for the longest time. Finally, Gerald did. "What exactly are you trying to do? We're only doing this 'cause we have no choice."

At least he talked. Mikey was determined to keep his mouth shut until Gerald said something. Anything. "Under his breath. "I'll take whatever I can get. Stay in control, Mikey."

So with that in mind, Mikey tried to make small talk. "Nice day, hey?" That was met by another grunt. And that's the way it went for the rest of their time together. "Ok, see you Friday, same time, same place. Enjoy the rest of your day." Another grunt from Gerald and they went their separate ways.

Doug, on the other hand, was waiting for Mikey to arrive. "Can we go back to the shelter today?"

"You bet. Like that place, hey?"

"Yeah. Especially the dogs. I like cats too, but I love dogs!"

"Wouldn't it be cool to be able to work in a place like that?" Mikey was probing.

"I'd love that. They don't care who you are. They just love you to death." Doug was in his own little world.

"Here we are. Tell you what, let me chat with Clara for a moment, and if she's ok with it, I'll leave you here for a couple of hours. Is that ok with you?" Mikey and Clara had already had this discussion but Doug didn't need to know that.

"Yeah, that'd be great!"

Mikey returned in a matter of minutes. "Clara says it would be fine with her but she'd like to get you to do a couple of chores while you're here. You ok with that?"

"Anything. Yeah, whatever she wants." Doug couldn't help but smile. "Thanks man!"

And with that, Mikey headed back to the church to confer with Pastor Rick. This was going great! When he picked up Doug, he actually had to wait for him. "Sorry about that. I wasn't finished cleaning up the back area. I didn't want to leave it for Carla. She's got enough to do."

As before, Doug talked the entire way back to the house. "See you Friday, Mikey. Thanks again!" Mikey could only shake his head. If Doug only knew where this was headed. Mikey wanted to tell him but it was still too risky, and from what he could tell, Gerald still held sway over Doug.

"Take it easy Mikey. Let it play itself out." Mikey loved talking to himself.

JANICE GOES TO BOCAS

"**O**K HON, IT'S ALL BOOKED!" Joline had been bugging Janice for weeks to book her trip to Panama. "Mom, I might not get accepted for a second semester, and then it'll be too late. You've got to see this place! It's really cool."

So with Joline's schedule in mind, Janice booked her flight. Joline would arrange accommodations as soon as she had her Mom's itinerary. Right down town, the Paridise Hotel backed onto the water. "Mom would like it here." She'd spent several days here herself while awaiting accommodation at the Institute. In the evening, she'd slip onto the outdoor patio just off the restaurant. They closed early, but she'd gotten to know the security guard/captain of his own tour boat, and he'd let her sit out there for hours. Plus he'd taken her to all of the cool places most operators didn't go to.

Less than half a mile away was the island of Bastimentos. The lights from Bocas and Bastimentos would play together on the waves that separated them. They had beckoned her come, and she had, on several occasions. "Mom, you're going to love it here!" Joline thought to herself.

Now that she had her Moms itinerary, she was able to make the arrangements. "Let's see. We definitely have to go to Boca del Drago. And Red Frog Beach. And of course, Bastimentos. This is the real

Caribbean, Mom! The music is incredible!" Talking to herself as usual. "I can't wait!"

Janice had thought about asking Mikey to accompany her but thought better of it. "It's going so well. Janice, slow down. You don't want to screw it up. And besides, I'll finally get time to spend time with my daughter, just the two of us!" All to herself, of course.

Mikey was as excited for her as she was. "Just go and enjoy yourself. Remember, look as much as you want, just don't touch!" He had laughed at that, but it really wasn't all that funny. "Crap. I miss her already and she's not even gone."

And finally Janice was on her way. It would be a long flight but taking the red eye made sense. That way she'd be in Panama City the next afternoon. Joline had already arranged a pick up for her so all she had to do was sit back, relax, practice her Spanish, at least a little, and read her newly acquired travel brochure.

They arrived at Tocumen as per schedule, passed through customs, and through the hordes of taxi drivers, until she spotted her name held aloft by one of the driver's. That was easy. She was tired but excited, and tried her best to engage the driver with her severely limited Español. Even the drive from the airport was cool. "Wow. I love it here already."

When the driver pulled up to the hotel, Joline was waiting. She handed the driver the appropriate funds, rushed to embrace her Mom, who was dying in the heat by this time, grabbed her luggage and headed for the air conditioned lobby. "My God, is it hot!" Indeed it is.

"Mom, maybe you should catch a couple of hours of sleep first, then we can go out for a late dinner. Ok?"

"Not a chance. I didn't come all the way here to sleep. Just let me grab a quick shower, and I'll be ready to go." Janice was having none of that.

"Ok, Mom. I'll head down to the lounge. It's just off the lobby. Join me when you're ready and we'll go from there."

Thirty minutes later Janice emerged, refreshed, and oh so ready to spend time with her daughter. A tall glass of very cold water would do the trick. Thank you very much. Or should I say, gracias. And off they strode . . . into the heat of the day. "My God, it takes your breath away. And my clothes already feel damp." All Joline could do was chuckle. There's no getting away from it. But, you'll adjust. Sooner or later.

Panama City is a city of immense contrasts. World class skyscrapers, architectural marvels, and slums galore. Old and new, side by side. And wonderful eating establishments. But the best of the best is the so called "typical Panamanian" local establishments, where the regular folk gather for authentic Panama grub.

Janice would experience the gamut for the next couple of days led by her daughter turned guide. And then they'd fly to Bocas rather than bus it since time was of the essence. Besides, Joline had someone she wanted her Mom to meet. But first she wanted to get her Mom settled into the Paradise Hotel and do a walk about of her adopted town.

Janice was impressed with her daughter's take charge attitude. One would never know that she'd only been here a short time herself. The locals greeted her as one of their own. Obviously Joline had done more than just work since she'd arrived here.

"Mom, I'm going to head over to the Institute for a few hours. You get settled in, and yes, it's safe to go wandering around. I'll meet you back here at 6, ok? I have someone I want you to meet. Bye." And with that Joline took her leave, not giving her now incredibly curious Mom time to respond.

Janice shook her head. "I should have known." And then a thought crossed her mind. "Stop that Janice! No assumptions, remember?" But to be honest, she couldn't stop the thought that had crept in. "I wonder if it's a male or a female?"

So of course Janice became more and more nervous as 6 o'clock approached. "Janice, it doesn't matter. Just calm down. Breathe." And that's when the phone rang. "Hello."

"Hi Mom, I'm down in the lobby. Whenever you're ready, come on down. No rush."

Janice checked her hair one more time, took a deep breath and headed down the stairs. Joline was all alone. "Ok." Under her breath.

"Capitan Caribe is just a couple of blocks away. We go there a lot. I bet you'll love it."

"Sounds good to me. Is your friend meeting us there?" Janice couldn't help herself.

Joline smiled to herself. She knew her Mom was dying to ask her about her friend. But she loved keeping her Mom on edge. "I might have to ask a shrink about that some day."

"Yes, hopefully soon. Here we are. Pretty cool place, hey?" And that was the end of that conversation.

A couple of drinks later, Joline suddenly stood up. "Hi babe. I want you to meet my Mom."

"Mom, this is Abbas. We work together at the Institute."

Before Janice knew it, Abbas had wrapped his arms around her and gave her a quick peck on each cheek. "I'm so glad to finally meet you." And then he sat down.

"And I'm very glad to finally meet you as well. Joline has told me absolutely nothing about you." That's when Janice bit her lip. "Oh crap! I did it again." To herself this time, but as usual, too late.

Joline and Abbas exchanged glances, and then burst out laughing. When Joline finally got herself under control, she let her Mom in on her little secret. "I'm sorry Mom, but I knew you'd blurt out something. I'd already warned Abbas to be ready for anything. See, Abbas, I told you."

"You really know me, don't you, you little brat! I'm mad at you." Janice feigned anger as best she could but that was a lost cause, and soon she was giggling right along with these two crazy people. "I'd like another drink, please."

So that's how Janice met Abbas. And that's when she found out just how serious the two of them were.

ERIN AND SYLVIA

ERIN KNEW SHE WAS taking a huge risk having Janice's Mom meet Sylvia but she felt that she didn't have a choice. Janice had practically adopted her. And she hadn't judged her. Erin was mature enough to know that not everyone, in fact, most would not embrace her lifestyle. Even she struggled with it. And like it or not, Joline had led her to the Lord. She loved that fact but it opened up a huge can of worms as well. She'd even met with Pastor Rick on several occasions to talk about it. "I know God loves me but . . . " She knew she'd have to reconcile this somehow or other. Sylvia went to church as well and her church had embraced her. "It's so confusing! I don't want to change churches but I may not have a choice. I need to talk to Pastor Rick some more." All to herself.

Sylvia knew she was gay from an early age. Her parents had tried to suppress it but it became overwhelmingly apparent as she hit puberty and beyond. She'd been brought up in a Christian home and knew her parents loved her, but she also knew she'd never fit in. And that's when she left their family church. She'd prayed mightily to this God she knew. She knew He loved her, in fact, never even questioned his love. But still she was reviled by those who called themselves Christians, those same people who said they believed that God was love. But apparently love was just for certain people, and not the degenerates like her. Thank God she was intelligent enough to understand that the God of the Universe loved her just as much as anyone else. That's what she'd hang onto. And she'd even learn to love the haters through the person of Jesus Christ.

That's how she'd survive in this fallen world. So she held her head high, and with determination and guts, and lots of hard work, she rose to prominence in the financial field, and now sat as a councillor at city hall as well. She'd earned her stripes, taken her lashes, all the while watching the moral decay around her. She found it incredibly interesting how certain "sins" held so much more prominence than others. Funny, she'd understood from her reading of the gospel that all fell short, not one among you is innocent. She'd carry her own cross; the one God had assigned her, and she'd let them carry theirs.

But then she'd walked into that bistro, and she'd met the owner, Erin. And that's when her life changed. And Erin's.

CLAIRE MAKES HER MOVE

CLAIRE KNEW THE TIME was coming when she'd be leaving Seattle. She'd better start saying her good byes soon, just in case it happened sooner rather than later. The best place to start was with Mom and Dad. What incredible people they were! She'd felt like the prodigal daughter when she'd finally found her way home. She'd treated them and Janice so badly, and yet they'd stretched out their arms to her when she'd finally returned. Sadly, she was about to leave yet again, but this time she'd keep in touch. "I promise."

They fawned over her as usual. She had intended on this being a short visit but they'd have none of that. "Claire, you're staying for dinner. Don't argue with me. We don't get to see you very often. And call Derek so he can join us. Dinners at 6 and tell him we won't take no for an answer. So that's what happened. When they spoke, everyone listened. But finally the evening ended. Claire and Derek said their good nights and headed out to the driveway.

Even that was becoming awkward. "Just so you know, I'm heading to Portland for a couple of days on assignment." Claire broke the impasse.

"Ok, no problem. See you at home." And with that, Derek drove off.

Claire stood there for a moment longer until his tail lights disappeared. She finally got in her vehicle, fastened the seat belt, and reluctantly headed home. "Home. Yeah right. I wish I knew where it was."

When she awoke the next morning Derek was already gone. "Just as well." Under her breath. This was awkward enough. Last night was painful. "We've gotta deal with this real soon."

And with that Claire headed to Portland. And the further south she drove the happier she became. "I'm free!" Guilt was no longer a factor. But now it was time to get down to business. Her contact had gathered the rest of the info she needed and an hour from now she'd have everything she needed to bring Richard down.

But as the miles ticked off Claire's mind kept wandering to the gun she carried in her bag. Self talk wasn't helping a whole lot. "Claire, forget it. Do the right thing." But even as she spoke the words she pulled the 45 from her purse. "He deserves it; he deserves to die!" By now she was scaring herself. "It's his own fault. Threatening my family? How dare you!" Anyone seeing her like this would have been frightened. She wore it for all to see. Thank God she was driving, for she was not a pretty sight to behold.

She quickly put the gun back in her purse. "My God, Claire, what the hells got into you?" She'd even scared herself. "Holy crap!"

He was waiting along the boardwalk as per their arrangement. At least she paid well. Hell, he'd work for her anytime. He'd checked her out a long time ago. She was one tough broad according to his sources. Don't cross her. So he didn't, and any info he passed on to her was guaranteed to be accurate. After all, he was a businessman, and a damn good one at that. He just liked cash. Who doesn't?

So now she had everything she'd ever need to put this slime ball away, that is, if she decided to. She wasn't too sure about that yet. Or if she could carry through with the other. But for tonight, she'd hit the lounge for a few drinks and leave that decision until tomorrow.

DEREK SEES HIS LAWYER

WHAT COULD IT HURT? It was pretty obvious that they were headed down the road to oblivion. Might as well be prepared. But it was still embarrassing. And the lawyer was his friend. Derek shook his head, sucked it up and walked into his friend's office. "Hi Jerry."

"Hey Derek, what's up? We could've met somewhere for coffee. Why don't we slip out of here for a bit? I'm buying."

"No Jerry. I need to talk to you privately. Sorry, but I'm kinda strung out."

Jerry had never seen Derek this way. "Yeah, of course. Sit down. What's on your mind?"

So Derek spilled his guts. For the next half hour. Finally, he stopped. "God, I'm sorry I dumped on you like that. Now I'll shut up." But he didn't, and now Jerry was getting worried.

"Derek, have you talked to anyone else about this? Rick or Mikey or anyone? You need to, man."

Of course he was right. But for now, it was Jerry. And of course Jerry would fill him in on all his options. He was his lawyer, but more importantly, he was his friend.

"Have you even spoken to Claire about this?"

"Not yet. But we avoid each other like the plague. I know she's thinking the same thing. I know her."

"Ok Derek. I'll put together something for you, but please talk to Claire first. And the Pastor."

Derek really didn't want to talk to Mikey about this, after all, Claire was his sister. But even as he thought that, he knew Mikey would be hurt by his omission. He could already hear him. "I thought we were better friends than that. Come on man!" Maybe he'd better rethink that.

As for the Pastor, they'd been close for years but this was downright embarrassing. My God, he'd just married them less than 2 years ago! And Rick even knew about the adoption fiasco, and now this. Crap!

And when he and Claire actually sat down to discuss their "marriage," he knew where that'd go real fast.

CLAIRE'S REVENGE

WHEN CLAIRE RETURNED TO her room later that evening, slightly inebriated, her plan was to crash for the night and then get down to business the next day. But that's not quite how it worked out. Sleep was evasive and her mind incredibly active, and not about her prey either.

No, her mind was on Derek. How could their marriage gone from love and kisses and adopting babies to this? To nothing. Maybe the whole fairytale thing was just that. A fairytale. She'd been absolutely sure that she'd loved him, at least to the extent that she could love. Maybe that was it. Maybe she was incapable of really loving anyone. "I guess I could be like everyone else and blame my parents. Like that'd do any good." And upon further reflection. "And why would anyone love me when I'm so inconsiderate of them? What's wrong with people?" Claire was having her own version of a meltdown. "They'd all be better off without me!" So why the tears, Claire? What's that all about?

It would be a rough night for Claire. "Maybe something will go wrong tonight, and he'll get me instead of me getting him. Then it'd be over." And with that, Claire knew exactly what her mode of operation would be this night. She walked over to her purse, removed the 45 and laid it on the table. She checked the side pocket of her purse for bullets. Yep. Ditto for the gloves. Now all she'd need was the guts to follow through. And anyone who knew her knew she had plenty of those!

Still, regardless of what happened this night, she would have to make sure she told absolutely no one. Just one problem, her snitch would know exactly what went down, or at least have a very good idea. And he could talk to someone. Not good. Perhaps they'd better have a little chat.

Finally the day yawned and bade all goodnight. And that's when the night crawlers appeared, she among them. He wasn't hard to find and soon the stalker was now the stalked. If he stuck to his MO, he'd be falling down drunk in a few hours from now. He'd most likely head over to his favourite hookers establishment as usual, and an hour later, he'd attempt to drive himself home. Hmmm. Nice car. Someone would kill to get their hands on it, I bet. We'll see.

Richard did exactly as his profile suggested he would. Claire surveyed his every movement from the sanctity of her own vehicle. And finally he emerged from the house, plunked himself down in the Ferrari and sped away, Claire in hot pursuit.

Out of town. Perfect. Finally he slowed down to a crawl and pulled into a driveway blocked by a large gate. Damn! I can't follow him in there. But no, something was wrong with the gate. He's getting out of the car and trying to punch in the numbers on the control panel. It's now or never!

She'd killed the lights and the motor so he didn't hear her approach. She had already slipped her gloves on in anticipation. The 45 felt good in her hands. "Stay calm, Claire. Steady." And then she raised her hand, steadied her wrist with the other hand, and pulled the trigger. Twice. One in each leg. She said not a word as she slowly retreated to the shadows hiding her vehicle. She started the engine and slowly drove away.

"She tried to block the screaming from her ears but she could not. "That'll teach you, you psycho!" Cold, Claire, cold.

She stopped only once on the journey back to the hotel. The water was deep, the gun unregistered and devoid of identification anyway. "Goodbye friend." And with that she sent it to a watery grave. The next stop would be her hotel. She ordered up a bottle of wine, ran the soaker tub, and laid back contemplating her next move. But first, she'd savour what had been an exceedingly great evening. Maybe she'd found herself a new career. And with that, she toasted herself until the bottle of wine was no more.

MIKEY'S MISSING JANICE

"**G**OD, I MISS HER." Mikey mouthed to himself. "I sure hope she's having a great time with Joline. I'm glad she didn't invite me along. They need to spend some time together." That's what he said but what he was really wondering was why the heck haven't I heard from you yet? It's been 3 days!

Janice really wanted to call Mikey to tell him how much she missed him, and of course, to fill him in on everything that was going on down here. Especially about Joline and Abbas. But she had resisted. After all, he was the one that told her to go have some fun with your daughter, just not too much. She had to giggle at that. If he only knew how much she wanted him here with her.

But of course, that's why she didn't call him. She knew she'd break down and plead with him to get down there right away, and he probably would. Then what? Nope, better to play it safe. She'd be heading home in 4 days from now anyway.

Mikey remembered telling Janice that she should just turn off the phone, enjoy herself but call when she was leaving so he'd know when to pick her up. She'd protested. "It'll be the middle of the night. I can take a cab. You don't need to do that." But he'd insisted. And of course, that's exactly what she wanted, to see him waiting for her on her arrival. She'd have to write a scene like that into one of her books. He'd swoop her into his arms and say something totally romantic like

91

"I'll never let you leave me again" or something equally inane. She giggled at the absurdity of it.

But thankfully it was a busy time for Mikey. Besides the rather intense schedule with Gerald and Doug, he had full times duties at the church. And when the economy sucks, like now, there are a whole lot of hurting people around, and as usual, prayer and the church become the last resort instead of the first. But at least we're here, thank God for that!

"I just wish Janice would call!"

DEREK TALKS TO MIKEY AND RICK

EREK DECIDED TO FOLLOW Jerry's advice. First Rick. They'd been close forever and even though Rick was his Pastor, he called on his friend, Rick, not Pastor Rick.

"Derek, I know you. Maybe you know how to read people but so do I. That's my job. Do you think anyone comes in here and tells it like it is? Rarely. I listen, I watch, and I read between the lines, where most of the information really is. Just like you do, right?"

He had to agree. He did that all the time. But this was different, or was it? Hadn't he been analyzing Claire the whole time? He knew damn well that she was analyzing him. Hell, she was a master at it! Come to think of it, so was he.

He had to chuckle. If I was a writer here's what I'd write. "Derek and Claire sat across from each other the entire evening, neither saying a word. But when they retired for the night they knew all there was to know about the other. This would go on for 10 years, both afraid to open their mouth less they say the wrong thing." And now there was one less decade to worry about.

There was no way he'd let that happen. He'd have "the chat" as soon as she got home. 2 years felt like 10 already! Forget that!

"I think I'll grab a drink." Muttering to himself. "Nothing to hang around here for."

But of course that wasn't a wise move. He was already down in the dumps and a couple of drinks would be guaranteed to take him even further into the pit. But he went anyway.

She spotted him as soon as he walked in. "Hi Derek. It's been awhile." Millie sat nursing her drink. She wasn't much of a drinker, but it was so damn lonely at home with just her and the cat.

Perfect timing or terrible timing? Derek wasn't sure what to think. He liked this woman. If only he'd met her first! Still . . . "Hi Millie, may I?" He motioned to sit.

"Of course. Alone again, I see. Wife out of town again?" If Derek thought she sounded rather harsh, well, she was. "Men!"

He just nodded, ordered a beer, and hung his head. Millie softened immediately. "Come on, let's grab a booth." So that's what they did. As usual, they engaged in small talk until they'd exhausted that subject, which took about 5 minutes. "Derek, talk to me. You know I'm here for you, don't you?"

Of course he did. And if he was being honest with himself, he'd secretly prayed that Millie would be here tonight. "Derek, be careful. You're still married. Take it easy." All to himself of course.

But the timing was right, and our detective couldn't shut his mouth this night. Everything he'd been feeling towards Claire came tumbling out, and to his dismay, he blurted out his feelings for Millie. "Oh my God, I'm so sorry. I shouldn't said that." Too late. What's done is done.

Millie reached across the table and stroked Derek's hand. "Derek, I feel the same way about you, but until you deal with your situation, I can't get involved with you. I can be your friend. But just your friend. Understand?"

He could only nod. He knew she was right. What he didn't know was how close to the surface his feelings were. He'd better head home now. Millie would do the same. "I'll see you at the precinct tomorrow, ok?" And with that Millie walked out the door.

A few minutes later, Derek did the same, but not before he called Mikey. Even at this late hour, Mikey was available. "I always have time for whoever needs me. Especially you." These two had become close. Tragedy can do that to people.

They'd agreed to meet at the church. Just in case this discussion went for awhile. It did. All night. Two warriors discussing their feelings. Real men with real feelings. And now they were both exhausted. Too bad. It was time to get ready for work.

THE ALPHA AND THE PUP

GEORGE WAS EVEN QUIETER than usual when Mikey picked him up. Something had obviously happened but Mikey decided to play it cool. "Let him talk in his own time, Mikey. Don't say anything." Under his breath. But, George had nothing to say, and that went on for the next 2 hours. They walked in silence, neither giving an inch. "Fine, I can outlast you." Mikey wasn't liking this one bit!

When they pulled into the House parking lot, George grunted, got out and headed indoors. Mikey sat there for a few minutes deciding whether he should check in with the house master or let it pass. He decided on the latter. "So it goes. I knew this wasn't going to be easy." It was frankly, beginning to look like a lost cause.

"Hopefully it goes better with Doug." Mikey never stopped talking to himself. In any case, he'd be seeing Doug around 1 o'clock. At least he was making progress with him!

When Mikey arrived to pick up Doug, he immediately noticed that he was limping badly. But when he got in the car, there was no place to hide. Doug was a mess. "What the hell happened to you?"

But Doug was in no mood to talk. In fact, there was nothing Mikey could do to engage him. "Ok, Mikey. Take it easy. Grab a couple of coffee from the drive through. Drive around town. Give it time." Mikey thought to himself.

So that's what they did. It was obvious what had went down, given Gerald's surly attitude this morning. If he could get Doug to spill the beans, he'd do something about it. Real quick. "But first, I need you to step up." To himself of course.

On impulse, Mikey decided to swing by the animal shelter. "I just have to chat with Carla for a moment, ok?" Not a word from Doug. But when they got there, he could tell that Doug was perking up, a least a little. "Look around if you want." And with that, Mikey headed to Carla's office.

And that's when Doug opened the car door, struggled to his feet and headed to the door of the shelter. Carla and Mikey watched the monitors as Doug made his way from animal to animal, and then over to his "buddy" Buddha, a veteran of the shelter. He'd come to them in major distress, with injuries that would have fallen a lesser animal. Part pit bull, part Rottweiler, and ugly as sin, he would never be adopted out. Instead he'd become a mascot of sorts. And lately, Doug's buddy. Like now.

And that's how it stayed until it was time to head back to the house. Now Doug was ready to talk. More correctly, he was ready to answer a few questions. It didn't take long to confirm Mikey's suspicions. "Doug, this isn't over. Hang in there, ok? I have an idea. And don't say anything to Gerald. Nothing. Got it?" Doug nodded, and as he slowly extracted himself from Mikey's car, he mouthed "Thanks, man!"

Mikey drove a block up the street to ensure he was not visible to anyone at the house. He turned off the ignition, bent his head over the steering wheel . . . and cried. A few minutes later, a different Mikey emerged; a determined, problem solving man. "Things are going to change around here. Mark my words!" For absolutely no one to hear. Except him and God. And that's all that would be required.

PORTLAND ON THE PHONE

EREK WASN'T QUITE SURE what he was hearing. A detective he'd never heard of was asking him about his wife. "Excuse me. What do you want to know about my wife? And why?"

That's when he got the whole explanation, or at least as much as the detective was willing to divulge. "I'm sorry I can't tell you more, but the victim refuses to talk. In fact, I'm just playing a hunch. I only called you to prevent this getting out of hand. I'm assuming you'd rather talk to her rather than us doing it."

"Yeah, of course. I'll get back to you." And with that Derek hung up the phone. "Claire, what the hell have you gotten into this time?" He almost felt guilty thinking that, but with Claire, anything was possible. And in Portland, no less. "Isn't that where she thought her stalker might be from? He'd mentioned a shooting. There's no way that could be her. I'd know if she had a gun, surely to God!" The thoughts swirled in Derek's mind.

That's when he got Claire's text. "Hi babe, I'll be home around 7. Love you!"

Now what? And that's when he wished he was more like Claire. I should text her and tell her that I have an assignment out of town for the next few days. "See you when I get back." But of course he didn't. "Ok, Derek, tonight's the night. Deal with it head on."

On impulse, he texted her back. "Meet you at the usual spot for dinner. Nothing in the house to eat anyway." One thing at a time.

Derek arrived early. A couple of courage boosters would help. He shook his head ruefully. "Me, the great detective; a master interrogator afraid to confront my wife, the pit bull. Oh my God! "Did I just say that?" He looked around lest anyone heard him. Have another drink, Derek. Come on, little man.

She strode into the room as if she owned it. She was a stunner, no doubt about it. She knew it, too. "Hi baby, I missed you so much!" Sure you did, Claire. "I bet I could've made it as an actress." Perhaps the only person you're fooling is yourself, Claire. Just a thought.

"Hi hon." Derek was no better. "Cool it Derek, there's no rush. Let her talk." And that's what he did. And that's what she did. On and on. About nothing. Especially nothing about Portland. Ok, Claire.

So Derek, being the man he was, decided to put off the discussion until tomorrow. Made sense to him, after all, she'd just returned from a trip, it was late, the discussion would probably turn nasty. Yep, tomorrow made more sense.

They had arrived separately, and they now left separately, bound for the same destination, the house at the end of the street. It used to be the home at the end of the street. Time changes everything.

But they'd still keep up the pretence and play house this evening, like countless others were also doing. And no doubt, before they fell asleep for the night, they'd tell the other that they loved them. Then they'd each roll over to their side of the bed, and for the next two hours lay awake wondering what the hell happened to their perfect life.

BUT MOM, I REALLY, REALLY LIKE HIM

ABBAS JOINED THEM FOR A bite and some small talk before leaving the two of them alone. "Gotta go. Sorry, but I've got a ton of prep work to do tonight. We're leaving by 5 am for a three day expedition. So glad I got to meet you. Have fun while you're here. I'll see you when I get back." And with a quick hug for Janice, and a much longer one for Joline, he headed back to the Institute.

"Ok, Mom, he's gone. Start talking." Joline knew her Mom well.

Janice, cautiously. "He seems nice. Is it serious?" Might just as well jump right in the deep end. "Have you met his parents yet?"

"He's really nice Mom. And he's such a gentleman." Joline was just getting warmed up. "And he's funny, and so smart. I really, really like him Mom."

Janice drew Joline closer to her. She'd never seen her like this. Ever. This was serious. Perhaps there'd been enough talk for this night. "Why don't you show me around town. You said it's safe to walk around, right? Come on." And with that, Janice motioned the server over, paid the bill, and then they headed out on a walk about. Arm in arm.

"Hon, I know more about this place than you think."

"About Bocas? How could you? You've never even been to Panama, have you?"

"No, but I know someone who has. A good friend, actually. I probably know things about this place that you don't even know." Janice was definitely hustling her now.

"Mom, you're spoofing me, aren't you?"

"Me? I don't spoof. You're the spoofer, not me. But, I am a writer, and so is my friend; and he stayed in Bocas for several months, if I recall correctly. You still don't believe me, do you?"

Joline wasn't sure if her Mom was on the level or not. "Ok, Mom, tell me something about Bocas that I don't know."

"Ok, I will. You know that boat parked out by the Paradise Hotel, the one that says Captain Gabriel on the side of it?"

Joline was starting to perk up. Janice knew she was getting her attention now. "Well, he knows my friend. In fact, my friend told me to ask for him, if we wanted to go snorkelling, or whatever. And that he'd take us to places that the tourists don't normally go. And did you know that about 8 or 9 years ago that there were a series of murders all within a year in this area?" Janice was about to go on until Joline intercepted her.

"You're serious, aren't you? Oh my God! Ok, Mom, let's go find your Captain Gabriel right now."

Now it was Janice's turn to squirm. "God, I hope he told me the truth. He is a writer, after all, so who knows?" All to herself.

Bocas is not a large town, and within 20 minutes they saw said boat anchored right next to the hotel. Even Joline was starting to get excited. "Come on, let's find Captain Gabriel."

"Hola, Captain Gabriel!" And that's when they heard his retort. "Si?"

Interesting. Joline took charge now. "Are you Captain Gabriel?"

"Si. What can I do for you, señorita?"

That's when Janice butted in. "Sir, a friend of mine told me to look for you. He said that you'd take us out snorkelling, and maybe even help us find some sloths. He was here a few years ago. He's from Canada. His name was Duane. He's a writer and photographer. He said you'd remember him. I think it was in 2011.

"Ah. Señor Duane. Si! I remember him well. How is he?"

"The last time I talked to him he was doing really well. He does a lot of writing, and photography. He asked me to look you up. He said that you'd take really good care of us, and to let you know that he expects to be back in Bocas this year." Janice was beginning to feel pretty darn smug. And Joline was becoming a believer real fast.

But she still had to ask."Is it true that there were a bunch of murders that took place around Bocas around 2010 or so?"

"Si! It was a strange time. Every stranger that came here was under suspicion. Sorry, my English is not so good."

"Your English is fine. So it's all true, Mom! You're a rock star. So, Captain, can we book you for a few trips over the next couple of days?"

"Si, señorita. Please tell mi amigo "hola from Gabriel. Gracias. Tomorrow morning at 9 at the Paradise Hotel. Si?"

"Si, señor. Gracias."

And that's how the evening would end. It was getting late, and now they had a date to go snorkelling in the morning. Joline might just have to look this writer dude up on Amazon. "I wonder how well Mom knows this guy?"

Janice, on the other hand, was feeling oh so good! "But tomorrow, Joline, I want to know all about Abbas." To herself as usual.

MIKEY'S MOVE

MIKEY HAD SEEN HIS FAIR share of bullying while on the inside. And he'd seen a whole lot of it since he got out as well. Except that most of it was corporate bullying. And in the church? Definitely, but it was usually more subtle, but very real. He'd shook his head on so many occasions that he was afraid of ending up with a permanently stiff neck.

He'd learned to bite his tongue, but damn near swallowed it on a couple of occasions, when things got really bizarre. Still, he'd learned which battles he could fight now, and which battles would take a longer, more strategic approach. And he'd learned to start with prayer instead of saving it as a weapon of last resort. Amazing how that can change the outcome.

Of course, truth be known, Mikey would have much rather met Gerald in the alley out back for a little one on one. Then we'd see how big of a man you really are! But Mikey knew he couldn't go there. Instead, a quick call to the parole officer in charge of Gerald's file just might be enough. And if he needed backup, Derek was always more than willing to pull a few strings.

"Can we move Gerald to another facility? Or Doug? I want them separated. Do we have to jump through some hoops to make this happen or can we just do it?" Mikey was not letting this pass.

"We probably could but I'll need some documents outlining the reasons why a move is required. Plus, there needs to be space available in one of our other homes. You realize, of course, if any of these guys violate their parole, they could be sent to the slammer. Sounds like that's a real possibility. That might be the easier way." To say the Parole Officer was a little cynical was an understatement.

"I know that. I don't want it to come to that if I can help it. Doug has a real good chance of rehabilitation so I want to keep working closely with him. Gerald, I'm not so sure, but I'm not giving up on him just yet. But one or the other has to be moved. Sooner the better." Mikey would get his way one way or the other.

"Ok, leave it with me. I'll get back to you by day's end. I can't just snap my fingers and make it happen, you know? Well, maybe I could, but . . . I'll call you, get out of here so I can work on this thing!" The officer just shook his head. "These preachers are all the same. They think they can save everyone of these guys. Oh, well. He'll learn."

Mikey knew the recidivism rate was alarming in these kinds of situations but that didn't mean he shouldn't try. Besides, those were just numbers, and the ones he was working with actually had names. Big differences, but he had to admit. "I'm still naive enough to believe I can make a difference." You go for it, Mikey.

He wanted to call in the troops but decided to give the Parole Officer some time to do his job. Mikey wasn't impressed with the Officer's attitude but he had to admit, the Officer had been dealing with these "subjects" a whole lot longer than he had. "Bite your tongue, Mikey. He said he'd be back to you by the end of the day. Patience, my friend, patience." Mikey decided to go for a drive.

The call came sooner than expected. "I have to hand it to you. You're obviously doing something right. They've agreed to take Gerald off your hands but they've also requested a meeting with you tomorrow. Around 2 pm at their house. I'll give you their number." And with that, the Officer hung up.

Mikey quickly called to confirm the meeting. He was assured that on the completion of the meeting, they'd make arrangements for Gerald to be transferred to their facility. Perfect. Now as long as Doug kept his mouth shut and stayed away from Gerald for one more night, this should all go smoothly.

And it nearly did. That is, until Doug took exception to the way Gerald had treated him, and laid a whipping on him. If that wasn't bad enough, the staff said he kept threatening to kill Gerald if he even so much as looked at him sideways.

So of course, Mikey was called, along with the police. But if Mikey hadn't been as forward looking as he was, Derek wouldn't have arrived when he did, and Doug would've been spending the next several months locked in a cell. Instead, Derek took over and in his inimitable way, diffused the situation.

"We'll take it from here. Doug's coming with us. He won't be back." And with that, he hauled Doug into the backseat of his own vehicle and drove off. Mikey followed, and as soon as it was safe to do so, Derek pulled over, strode to the back door and opened it. "Get the hell out of my car! Now!" Doug wasn't sure if he should move or not. And that's when Mikey drove up.

"Get out!" Doug felt a little safer now that Mikey was here. So he extracted himself as best he could. Derek slammed the door behind him to ensure he got the point.

Mikey motioned Doug to his already opened door on his car. "Get in Doug." Then he went to talk with Derek. Derek was livid. Tread lightly Mikey. Which he did.

"I'm only going to say this once. The next time one of your "projects" goes sideways, don't call me. Got it?" Derek was incensed.

This wasn't the time to chat. "Got it. Thanks." Enough said, and besides, he now had Doug to contend with for the whole night. Crap! Fortunately, Doug was smart enough to keep his mouth shut. All he could think of was " I screwed up again!" And he had. Big time.

Since this was all on the down low, Mikey couldn't call the half house. Doug would be staying with him for the night. Great! He really didn't want Doug to know where he lived, obviously, so decided to head for the church. They'd always maintained a small suite in the basement for emergency use. It was rarely used but it would have to do for tonight. Thank God it was equipped with a couple of sofas, as well as a microwave, table and chairs, and so on. Plus there was a bathroom down the hall. This would be their home until tomorrow. "Thanks a lot Doug!" Under his breath. "Good night!"

DEREK CONFRONTS CLAIRE

S O NOT ONLY DID DEREK have to put out Mikey's fire, which put him in a surly mood, but now he had to deal with Claire. Crap! Maybe he should just slip out early and deal with it later.

And that's probably what he would've done, except Claire had decided she needed to have "the chat" with Derek before he headed off to work. Better to get it over with. She let out a sigh and strode into the kitchen. They nodded at each other. Each poured themselves a cup of coffee. And both sat down. They both knew where this was going but neither spoke.

Finally, Claire found her voice. "Derek, we both know this isn't working." Ever so slowly. "We can't go on this way. You know it, and I know it. I'm sorry, Derek, but I can't do this anymore. I know you're not happy either." And that's where she left it.

Derek sipped his coffee, fidgeted ever so slightly, let out a deep breath and finally spoke. "I know. It's been killing me too. I know you're not happy. I know I'm not. And when the adoption fell through, I knew it was the end of us. Claire, I do love you, but I can't live like this. And it's pretty obvious that you can't either." Derek hung his head. This was it. The end.

Claire couldn't contain the tears that had involuntarily began to make a path from the corner of her eyes, down her cheek, and pool at the tip of her chin. She wiped them away with her sleeve but as quickly as she wiped them away, they would reappear. "Claire, stay strong. You can do this." To herself.

"Derek, I've already called my lawyer. I won't contest anything. All I want is my personal stuff. I'll be gone by this afternoon."

Derek was stunned. "You're leaving today? Just like that?"

Claire nodded her head. "Yes. I start my new job tomorrow in L.A. I'm on the plane this afternoon. I'm sorry Derek." And with that, she got up and returned to their bedroom. Their bedroom. By late afternoon, it would just be

"his bedroom."

Derek wasn't prepared for this. He knew it was coming. Sometime soon. Just not right now. And he still had to talk to her about Portland. Forget that! If they wanted to talk to Claire, then go right ahead. I want no part of it.

"What now? I don't know what to do. What the hell did I expect to happen?" Derek finally stood, unsure of what to do next, then finally decided he needed to get out of there. Now. And even when he got in his car, he just sat there. Finally, he started the engine, put the vehicle in gear, and drove off. To where? He had no idea.

"I need to talk to Rick. That's what I'll do." That's when he realized that his phone was ringing. "Hello."

"Hey Derek, it's Jim. There's a detective here from Portland waiting for you. He said he didn't have an appointment but that he was quite sure you'd see him. He's been here for awhile. You ok? Your calls kept going to voice mail. What should I tell him?"

"Tell him I'll be there in 20 minutes. Sorry. I forgot my phone at home this morning. Let me check the messages and then I'll be in." Like it or not, he'd be dealing with Claire one way or the other. "Ok Derek, pull yourself together."

CLAIRE'S TAKE

SEEING DEREK SLOUCHED OVER like that had nearly done her in. She wanted to rush to his side, wrap him in her arms, and never let go, but she dared not. It would only prolong what they both knew was inevitable. She knew he still loved her, and she knew she still loved him. But it wasn't enough. Maybe for him, but definitely not her. It was better this way. And now it was done.

She had kept her ear to the door, barely breathing, until she heard him leave the house. Then she made her way to the bed, and for the next 2 hours she cried uncontrollably until sleep finally forced itself upon her.

She awoke with a start, glancing at her watch. "Oh my God! I'm going to be late. Crap!" She headed for the shower, quickly dressed, gathered what she could together, and headed for the cab that had arrived 15 minutes prior. "Sorry Derek. I'll have to pick up my stuff later. And my car." She muttered to herself, and one slightly irate cab driver. At least she'd left Derek a note.

When she boarded the plane, Claire was already beginning to feel lighter, and when they reached elevation, with the help of a couple of drinks, she was feeling downright good.

"Finally, I can get on with my life!" And she toasted the complete stranger sitting next to her.

A couple of more drinks and Claire was feeling no pain. She hated what she'd had to do this morning, but they both knew it had to happen. And now maybe Derek would get on with his life. He deserved more than she could ever give him. "I actually thought I could do it. I should've known!" Her seat mate just nodded. To himself "whatever the crazy woman says, just smile and nod."

Claire may have thought she was in the clear and about to begin another chapter in her already crazy life. But not quite. Not yet anyway.

Meanwhile, back in Seattle, Derek was being given the third degree by his Portland counterpart. Claire may have been his wife, but what the detective was telling him, certainly wasn't the Claire he knew.

It was beginning to look like there was a whole lot more he didn't know about about this person he had shared his bed with these past couple of years!

TELL ME MORE ABOUT ABBAS

JOLINE WAS BEGINNING TO wonder if she should have told her Mom anything about Abbas. She sure was acting weird about it. "What's her problem? She knows I'm not going to do something stupid!" Joline was ticked at first, but then relented. Her Mom had been through a lot. More than anyone should ever have to deal with. My God, she'd been married to a serial killer! How could it get much worse than that?

Truth be known, Janice was worried. Apparently Abbas' parents had been here for a visit, and he hadn't even bothered to tell his parents about Joline. Why not? Did he have something to hide? Or was she an infidel in their eyes? An unbeliever? Janice could feel her body chill at the mere thought. Janice often spoke to herself, like now. "I'm not prejudice. But just because I'm not, doesn't mean that others aren't prejudice again us. And what if you have kids? How will they be raised? Or maybe he'll want to move you to Iran. What then?"

That's where Janice was coming from. And besides, she was the Mom, and Mom's can ask whatever they want to. So when Joline picked her up the next morning to go tripping with Captain Gabriel, she felt well within her right to ask her anything she wanted to. And she did.

At first Joline was taken aback by her Mom's bluntness, but she had to admit that her Mom had a few points that she'd better look into before this relationship got any more serious than it already was. Perhaps her Mom was right. "Holy Crap! Why didn't I think about this?" Joline was searching her memory banks for past conversations between her and Abbas. Had they talked about any of the stuff her Mom had brought up? Well, as soon as he got back from his expedition, they'd be having a very long, serious discussion.

"Baby, I'm sorry to lay this all on you, but I only want the best for you. It just scares me. I'm not trying to get all religious on you but I remember Mom and Dad's concern for me being "unequally yoked." I know it referred to a believer and an unbeliever, and the built in difficulties of that kind of union, but it's something I've always thought about. And especially because of our Christian faith. Abbas is a Muslim, isn't he?"

"I've never even heard him talk about religion, to be honest. He told me his family was Muslim, but we never actually talked about it. I guess we need to, don't we?"

"You do. It's important, honey. Especially if you're bringing children into this world."

That's where this discussion would end for now. Mom and daughter slipped their flippers on, adjusted their face masks, and surveyed the watery world that Captain Gabriel had so graciously presented to them. But they weren't done yet, and soon the Captain was maneuvering among the mangroves. "Senoritas, look." And that's when they saw the sloths, 2 of them, moving ever so slowly. He cut the engine, motioned them to move slowly to the centre of the boat, and then one by one, he handed each of them a sloth. They sat there in silence, stroking the coarse hair of these creatures, until the Captain signalled them go.

"Thank you so much. That was awesome!" Joline was beside herself. "Your friend was right, Mom. I'm definitely going to check him out!"

And that's when Captain Gabriel spoke up. "We have time for one more stop. Señor Duane came to the exact same place to see the poison dart frogs." And with that, he headed for an area close to Red Frog Beach on Isla Bastimentos. He docked the boat and led his guests to an area frequented by the tiny frogs.

"Here. Do you want to hold one?" He extended his palmed hand to Janice.

"I thought they were poisonous? Is it safe?"

"Si. Don't squeeze him, just hold him like this."

So she did, and Joline, as well. But when they got back to Janice's room later, Joline employed Google for a bit. "Mom, that frog we were holding has enough poison in him to kill 10 grown men. According to this, the more colourful they are, the deadlier they are. Mom, that frog was bright red. We could've died! Thanks a lot, Captain!"

IT'S ALL ABOUT YOU, DOUG

"THANK GOD THAT NIGHT'S OVER! My poor back!" Mikey rolled off the sofa that was at least 6 inches too short for his oversized body. He looked over at a still slumbering Doug, shook his head, headed for the can, and made himself as presentable as he could. The meeting was in an hours time. Now he had to figure out what to do with Doug while he was in his meeting. "Wait a minute. Carla won't mind, I'm sure." A quick call confirmed his suspicion.

Doug wasn't sure what was going on, only that he still wasn't in a cell. And now he was going to visit Buddha.

Mikey's meeting went well. Of course, the previous night's incident didn't come up, thank God. "You can bring Doug over as soon as you want. His rooms ready for him now. Just check in with us when you get here. And Mikey, we've heard about the work you're doing. Great job! If there's anything we can do to help, just let us know."

"Thanks guys. I really appreciate it. I'll bring Doug by in a hour or so. Thanks again." Mikey could barely contain himself as he made his way back to his car. "Yes!"

Mikey's mood had changed considerably in the last hour and that would certainly work in Doug's favour. But Doug knew he'd screwed up. Big time. So when Mikey came through the door, he headed out to meet him. "Mikey, I really screwed up. I'm sorry, man. I was just so pissed off at Gerald. I lost it. Im sorry. I promise you, it'll never happen again." He meant it, and Mikey knew he did. Carla watched the whole thing. This was all going to work out just fine.

A couple hours later found Doug in his new home. And no Gerald. So no excuses. If he screwed this up, it was over. "I'll do you proud, Mikey. Just wait and see." Doug even crossed his heart in a pledge to Mikey.

WHAT NOW DEREK?

EREK WAS DEVASTATED. This morning he was still married. Now, he wasn't. And she was so damn cold. He shivered at the memory. Oh yes, she'd cried, and then she'd surgically removed him from her life, as if he was some unwanted or unneeded appendage. Just like that. And now she was gone, and he didn't want to go home. So he didn't. He went to the bar instead.

Millie knew something was wrong the moment Derek walked in. He didn't say a word as he sat down at her table. She mouthed her order to the waiter, then waited until the drinks arrived before reaching out to hold Derek's trembling hands. That seemed to calm him somewhat. Finally, Derek spoke. "Claire's gone."

Millie heard the words but was unsure of what he meant. "Gone? On another trip?"

"No. It's over. Our marriage is over. She's gone." And with that he hung his head, and she could feel him sobbing, ever so gently.

She drew him even closer to her, and as much as she resisted, she could feel her tears welling up. He was such a good man. He didn't deserve this! And that's how they'd stay for the next couple of hours.

"Derek, let's get out of here. You're coming to my place. I won't take no for an answer."

He began to protest but to no avail.

"Don't worry. I have a spare bedroom. That's where you're going. But you're not staying alone tonight, and that's final!" Millie wasn't taking no for an answer.

Despite himself, Derek had to chuckle. "Yes ma'am. Whatever you say, ma'am."

"And quit being a smart ass!"

He couldn't help himself. He started to laugh. And cry. All at the same time, and soon she was doing the same.

"Waiter. Bill please." And with that, they were out of there.

ALPHA DOG NO MORE

GERALD KNEW SOMETHING WAS up when Doug didn't return to the house that night. He'd already heard through the grapevine that Doug hadn't ended up in a cell. That's where he deserved to be. "I'll get him if it's the last thing I do!" Gerald was pissed!

Mikey couldn't help but smirk when Gerald hobbled over to his vehicle, open the door and practically fall into the seat. "Rough night?" God, he was enjoying this. All Gerald could do was glare. Even putting on the seat belt was an ordeal.

Mikey wasn't done yet. "I thought that maybe we should go for a jog today. It's looks like you could use the exercise." Dig a little deeper, Mikey, man of God that you are. "Ok, Mikey. Enough!"

Gerald just stared at him. "You arranged this didn't you?"

"Excuse me? Arranged what?"

"I should report you." Gerald was not having a good time.

"You sent Doug on me. Are you crazy? He could've killed me!"

Mikey damn near laughed out loud. This so called alpha dog was just a pup. Big man until someone confronted him. Like most bullies! "Keep quiet Mikey. Let it pass." Which he did. And they decided not to jogging that day.

But now Gerald was troubled. God, he didn't want to ask Mikey anything, in fact, he wanted to be anywhere but near this guy, but he needed answers. So he sucked it up. "When's Doug coming back to the house?"

"He's not." Mikey was going to make him work for everything.

"Is he in jail?"

"Nope."

Silence is not always golden, and if Gerald's face was any indication, there was a storm raging real close to the surface. "Be careful Mikey, he could explode. Keep both hands on the wheel." Mikey gripped the steering wheel even tighter. One never knows." And that's when he decided to diffuse the situation a little.

He pulled into the drive through and ordered two large cones, passed one over to Gerald, and proceeded to cruise around. That's all it took to change the mood, and soon they were able to have a discussion of sorts. About everything except Doug, that is.

Gerald knew he was fighting a losing battle so decided to change it up a bit. "What's going to happen to me? I know you like Doug more than me. That's obvious." And that's when he thought it best he shut up.

Mikey bit his lip yet again. But at least Gerald had talked, even asked him a question. Now maybe they could get somewhere. "What do you want to see happen to you?" Let's throw it back at him. This could get interesting.

Gerald just stared at Mikey. "This might be my only chance." To himself. "Don't screw this up." And he didn't. So he told Mikey. "If I wasn't such a loser, I'd probably be a mechanic. I love working on vehicles." And that's when Mikey caught a glimpse of the real Gerald.

"Seriously? It's never too late, you know."

Gerald sunk back into the seat. "Yeah it is. With my record, no one would ever hire me, unless it was a chop shop or something. I kinda screwed that up a long time ago."

Mikey's mind was buzzing. "My God, was this actually happening? Could it be a breakthrough with this guy? Probe a little deeper." And he did. And that's when Gerald really started to open up.

By the time Mikey dropped him off, they'd gone an extra hour past their allotted time. Gerald had even waved at him when he drove off. "Thank you God!"

GET READY, LOS ANGELES

L ESS THAN 3 HOURS LATER, Los Angeles, the City of Angels, welcomed Claire into their midst. Twelve hundred miles from Seattle. Far enough to keep family away, but only three hours by plane when she felt the need to re-engage them on occasion. She'd sort of said her goodbyes last week, but she'd officially make the rounds when she picked up her vehicle and the rest of her stuff in a couple of weeks. By that time they'd all know that she and Derek were going their separate ways, and that she'd already moved on. Sorry. That's just the way it is.

Now it was time to check out her new home. She'd left out a couple of details when she and Derek had "the chat." She didn't actually have a job here yet, but since she was a freelancer, it wasn't technically a lie. And she didn't have a place to live yet, but that would be resolved in the coming days. At least she was out of Seattle. That was the main thing.

The hotel would do nicely for the next few days until she found a place to live. But she'd better get back to the horde of voice messages that she'd been neglecting the last couple of days. Especially the ones from the detective in Portland. He'd left at least 5 different messages all urging her to call him immediately upon receiving his message. "Fine. You're first." And with that she dialled his number. And thus would begin the game of cat and mouse between these two. And how Claire loved to play!

But on a more serious note, she'd better be extra careful. He hadn't told her what he wanted to talk about, just that they needed to meet, preferably in Portland. "Forget that!" If he wanted to meet that badly, he'd best jump on a plane and meet her here. He had nothing on her. She'd made sure of that.

Claire knew that her family would be devastated. That's why she'd left so quickly. The thought of them confronting her was more than she was willing to deal with. Everyone knows that Derek's a great guy. And that she has a wonderful family. Without question. Cliche or not, it's me guys, not you.

The next couple of days were a whirlwind for Claire. She loved L.A. This was the town she'd been missing! By the second day she'd found an apartment that would serve her needs perfectly. It even had a parking space. By week's end it was fully furnished except for the personal items she'd left back in Seattle. Like it or not, she'd be seeing Seattle a lot sooner than she wanted to. And Derek. And the family.

The phone buzzing in her hand snapped her back to the present. "Oh my God, it's him again!" Her detective friend. "Hello."

"Just thought I'd let you know that I took you up on your offer."

"What offer?" Claire was confused.

"That if I really wanted to talk to you, I'd have to come to L.A. Well, here I am. I'll text you the address of the hotel. Will 7 pm work for you? I'm heading back in the morning."

She had to admit that she liked his style. Kinda like hers. How could she refuse? So she didn't. But she added one caveat. "You're buying."

JANICE HEADS HOME

WHAT AN INCREDIBLE TIME she's had with Joline. But it was definitely time to go. God, she'd missed Mikey. And he'd be waiting for her when she got back. "I'm telling him exactly how I feel the moment I see him. I don't care if a thousand people see us. I love you Mikey!" Janice was absolutely giddy at the thought.

Joline watched as her Mom's plane lifted off the Tarmac on route to Panama City. The connections had worked out perfectly, and if everything went according to plan, Janice would be back in Seattle in the wee hours of the morning. And, she had to giggle at the thought, her Mom's Prince Charming would be waiting to scoop her into his arms and declare his undying love for his fair damsel.

"But, maybe I'd better deal with my own Prince Charming. Somehow, Mom's sounds a lot more exciting. Joline. Quit it! Give him a chance."

Abbas knew he was about to get the second degree and he wasn't liking it one bit. Why should he have to explain himself to her?" And that's when he realized what he'd been thinking. Crap! Suddenly Joline had all these questions and he didn't have answers. It hadn't even crossed his mind. And that's when he realized that he could lose her. He knew she loved him, she'd told him so. And he'd declared his love for her, but ever since her Mom arrived, things had changed. She even looked at him differently. He'd better get this figured out real fast!

So tonight would find Joline and Abbas having a long, drawn out discussion that lasted most of the night. And probably about the same time their discussion ended and they called it a night, Janice's plane touched down in Seattle, and moments later she was rushing into the arms of her Prince Charming. It would be days later before Janice would know whether Joline's night had ended in the arms of a Prince or a Frog.

MILLIE TAKES CHARGE

"**M**Y GOD, HE'S STILL SLEEPING." Millie had been up for hours already. "Thank God it's Sunday. Poor man." She resisted going into his room. That could lead to a whole lot of complications that were better left for another day. These two were close. Very close. If there was even a chance of a future together, this had to be handled right.

So instead she made breakfast. And then, as she was about to rap on his door, he emerged with a huge smile on his face. "Good morning! It smells great in here." And with that he gave her a hug and then followed his nose to the exquisite spread laid out before them. "Wow."

He was pleased, she even more so. "Coffee, fine sir?"

"Why, yes indeed. Thank you very much, madam." It was if a light switch had suddenly turned on. This was definitely not the Derek that had shown up here the previous night.

They drank multiple cups of coffee; they feasted on Millie's gourmet breakfast; they enjoyed the company of the other. No tension. No stress. No Claire. Perfect.

Unfortunately, reality has a habit of showing up, and soon Derek's mood began to change. They both sensed it so Millie agreed to drive Derek back to the pub to pick up his vehicle. She knew he didn't want to go, and he knew she wanted him to stay, but there were issues he had to deal with now. They'd have their chance later. Neither wanted to screw that up. But right now it was time to head home. And time to gather everything that was "Claire" and deposit in her vehicle, everything. And then he'd park her vehicle out in the driveway. And then he'd change the locks. "Good bye Claire! Good riddance!" And that's when he did a little dance.

Millie, on the other hand, didn't savour going home to a now empty house, so she decided to go shopping. It seemed that a few nice outfits just might be in order. One never knows when one might get asked out and she'd sure hate to be caught with nothing to wear!

THE MOL AND THE COP

CLAIRE DECIDED THAT SHE needed a long bubble bath before she met the detective for dinner. She stretched out like a Cheshire Cat as the bubbles followed the curves of her rather luscious body, making her look, and feel, oh so sexy. She starts to giggle. Like a Mol. In the gangster movies. A femme fatale. "Maybe that's what I'll become. A modern femme fatale." She immersed herself in her daytime dream world until the bubbles signalled their impending doom. "I know. I'll dress to the nines for our dinner tonight. That should confuse him." Don't get too cocky, Claire. Maybe you're not as smart as you think you are.

Even the cabbie couldn't take his eyes off her. She knew it, and every time their eyes met, he'd look away. She'd smile to herself. And for the rest of the trip downtown, she imagined herself as the ultimate hitman, or is that hitwoman? Whatever. Had the cabbie known that she'd used her hands as a would be gun, and his back as a target, he might have thought differently about the lady occupying the back seat of his cab.

She tipped him generously, leaning over ever so slightly as she emerged from the cab. He tried not to look but that proved to be impossible. As he drove away, she raised her hands ever so slightly, took aim at the fleeing cab, and gently pressed the imaginary trigger. In her minds eye the bullet found its mark, and as the cabbie slumped over the steering wheel, the vehicle veered into the path of the on-coming police car, flipping it on its lid. There would be no survivors this day. She turned and walked into the restaurant. It was time to meet the cop.

YOUR MOVE ABBAS

ABBAS HAD DONE SOME VERY deep soul searching the past couple of days. And it was a good thing because tonight's discussion would definitely be taking a toll on their relationship.

It started off casually with a couple of drinks, and the usual small talk, but both knew where this was headed. It didn't take long either until they were up to their knees in it. And it wasn't going particularly well for Abbas. His explanations, perhaps they should be called excuses, even sounded lame to him, and he was the one delivering them.

"My parents are kind of old school. You're white. And a Christian. And the way you dress. And . . . I never said I wanted kids." All over the place, but nonetheless drawing a very straight line, at least in Joline's mind.

The truth is, he'd never really thought about any of this stuff. Life was good. He had a great girlfriend. Not a care in the world. Until now. And she wasn't backing up one bit. He involuntarily shivered. She was looking right through him.

"Abbas, I'm tired. Maybe we can talk tomorrow, ok? I'm going to bed." And with that she got up and started walking back to the Institute.

"Hey wait! I'll walk with you." He hurriedly joined her. But there would be no more talk this evening.

He tried. "Nite hon. See you in the morning."

She barely nodded. There was really nothing to say. Or perhaps more accurately, everything had already been said.

Abbas texted her the next morning to let her know he'd be out at sea until late afternoon. Perhaps they could get together then. "Please give me a chance to explain. I really love you." There would be no response.

Once Joline was sure Abbas was indeed gone, she packed up all her gear, and then made a stop at the office to inform them that an emergency had just come up, and she'd have to leave immediately. And more than likely she wouldn't be back. Family stuff.

Of course they'd miss her. But such is life, and it wouldn't be hard to replace her. Not that she wasn't good at her job, just that they were constantly overrun with applicants. "Could you make sure Abbas gets this letter, please?" And that's when the cab arrived. She'd miss this place, and most of the people. But not all of them.

Joline wasn't sure what her next move would be, so rather than rush it, she'd head to Panama City for a couple of days. When she boarded the plane in Bocas, she knew she'd not be back. And then she turned off her phone, and she wouldn't be turning it back on until she was out of Panama.

Abbas must've send 50 texts to Joline that morning. Nothing. His mind was beginning to play games. Finally, they were back to the Institute. He rushed to her room. Not there. He searched the compound. Nothing. He asked the other staff members. No one had seen her. What the hell?

So he checked in at the office. They knew. "She had a family emergency. She left this for you." And that's when it really hit him.

He wandered down to their little hideaway on the beach just opposite the Institute, carefully opened the envelope, and prepared for the worst. The further he read, the more the tears flowed, and soon the remaining words were nothing more than a blur.

An hour later found him wandering aimlessly along the oceans edge. Around the same time in Panama City, Joline was slipping into a scalding hot bubble bath, glass of wine in hand, wondering what the hell had just happened to her perfect life.

CLAIRE MEETS ETHAN

C LAIRE HAD BEEN SO WRAPPED up in herself that she'd failed to spend time checking out her opponent. She should have. Ethan was no run of the mill cop. In fact, he'd spent most of his career right here in L.A. He'd stepped back from the edge several years prior, after a significant personal loss had threatened to derail him completely.

But when the "unknown assailant" case landed on his desk, with a rather infamous victim, he was all in. There was something about this particular case that spoke volumes to him. And anything that would take him out of self imposed exile was a very good thing.

So she walked into the lions den totally unprepared. That would be a first for her. Perhaps the known world didn't revolve around her after all.

He, on the other hand, had studied her file thoroughly, so recognized her easily when she arrived. Ever the gentleman, he quickly introduced himself and escorted her to the private booth especially reserved for this occasion.

Claire was decidedly not in charge on this particular occasion, but it was obvious that the chess game had begun. "My God, is he handsome!" Claire was Claire. "Ok, Claire. Smarten up. Get it together. Breathe." And she did. "Let him talk."

He'd been around a lot of very beautiful women during his time in L.A., and he'd seen it all. But he hadn't expected this out of Claire. Her M.O. suggested otherwise. She was known for her brilliance, and especially her pit bull, never back down, take no prisoners, work ethic. Not some over made up Barbie doll. Perhaps he didn't know as much about her as he thought. "Lead with a pawn, Ethan. Take it slow."

And that's how it went. They played the game slowly, each feeling the other out. Each sacrificed a pawn, and then another, as the game progressed. As the tension grew, and the sacrifices morphed into rooks and knights, it became apparent that this game would not end with an obvious winner this night.

Finally, with neither offering up further sacrifices, they decided to call it a draw. They'd be playing again. Sooner than later if Ethan had his way. Still, he now had a much better sense of his opponent. Obviously her "look" this evening was nothing more than a smokescreen meant to throw him off. It didn't work.

Claire poured herself a glass of wine while waiting for the soaker tub to fill. She absently added bubble bath, lit the candles which she'd placed around the tubs edge, and contemplated the evening just passed. "He's brilliant. And hot. Be very careful Claire." She spoke aloud to ensure she was getting her own message. "I know he has nothing on me. Nothing that would stand up in a court of law, for sure. Why's he so interested in this case anyway?" And with that, she killed the rest of the lights, and slipped into the oh so inviting tub.

But the night was far from over for Ethan. Time to head to his old precinct. He had some work to do, and he had a few friends that just might be working tonight. Old times. Good times. And besides, which he'd neglected to mention to Claire, he'd decided to stay in L.A. for a few more days.

BETWEEN A ROCK AND
A HARD PLACE

IKEY WASN'T QUITE SURE how he was supposed to feel. About Janice? That wasn't an issue. He loved her and she loved him. That part was perfect! The Parole Program with Doug and Gerald was proving to be a winner, thus far. In fact, headquarters wanted him to attend a meeting this very afternoon. The grapevine suggested it was nothing but good news! Great!

But then Derek confided in him, and that took the wind right out of his sails. He loved his friend, and he certainly didn't deserve the treatment he was getting. And to top it off, it was Claire delivering the body blows. My own sister! She didn't even tell me, and now she's left town without even saying good bye. All Mikey could do was shake his head. And pray.

That's when he glanced at his watch. Holy crap! The meetings in 20 minutes. "Smarten up, Mikey!" But of course he made the meeting. And the grapevine had actually got this one right.

"Mikey, we're hearing nothing but good reports on our little experiment. We've decided to expand it, and lengthen it as well. But of course, we'll need more people to work with the parolees, and we'll need a full time team leader. Do you know anybody who might be interested?" They exchanged glances among themselves.

"Are you offering me a job?" Take it easy, Mikey. "You know I work full time with my Church, right?" He wanted this real bad.

"We know. But would you be interested if we could figure out how to make it work, and still retain your position with your church?"

"Absolutely!"

"We were hoping you'd say that. In fact, we'd already taking the liberty and spoken to Pastor Rick this morning. We apologize if we've stepped out of bounds."

"No, that's fine. What did Rick say?"

"Why don't you ask him yourself." And with that, Rick emerged out of the shadows, strode up to Mikey, and gave him a huge bear hug. "I'm sorry to go above your head, Mikey, but it all happened so quickly. This is right up your alley!"

Mikey had to bite his tongue or he knew he was going to lose it. He nodded and finally he spoke. "I'd be honoured to be your man. Can I go now?"

"Go ahead. We'll be in contact shortly. Status quo for now. And Mikey? Thank you."

And with that Mikey headed straight to Janice's. She saw him running up the driveway. "Oh my God, something's happened!" She fling open the door but was totally unprepared when he grabbed her and began some crazy kind of chicken dance. "Have you lost your mind?" She swatted him. "Let me down!"

So he told her the news, and soon they were both doing the chicken dance. And the snoopy neighbour just down the way, well, even she closed the curtains. She needed to call . . . somebody . . . anybody.

But the good news would soon be shattered by the bad. He told Janice about Derek. And about Claire. And how disappointed he was in his sister. And how guilty he felt being so excited about the two of them, and about the new appointment.

They sat on the step lost in thought. "Mikey, we all make choices, some aren't so good, but they're ours. We'll be there for them when, or if they want us to be, right?"

He nodded. "You're right, of course. It's just so sad." And it was. But he just needed to be with Janice right now.

And forever.

DOUG AND THE DOG HOUSE

MIKEY DIDN'T WANT TO GET ahead of himself but it was going to be tough. Doug was waiting for him when he arrived, and when he saw Mikey, he knew something was up. Something good.

"You're shining. " Doug was a man of words.

"Excuse me? What'd you say?"

"You're shining, you know, like the sun."

Mikey shook his head. He knew what Doug meant, and damn it, he fully intended on sharing his sunshine with him. Why not? Except for that one rather unfortunate incident with Gerald, Doug was the main reason this program was going to another level. Damn rights he'd share it with him!"

"Doug. We need to celebrate!"

And now it was Doug's turn to question the sanity of the person sitting next to him. "Ok?" Cautiously.

"Doug, if you were a free man right now, where would you want to work?"

"Like anyone would ever hire me." Doug was being Doug.

"Forget that. Where would you work if you could?"

"That's easy. The shelter. I love spending time with the animals, especially the dogs."

"What if you could? I mean, have a job like that? Would you be able to handle it, or would you get bored and head back to the streets?" Mikey needed Doug's input.

"Man, if I ever get a job like that, I'd be there forever. I mean it!" And he did.

So Mikey offered up the carrot. "Doug, keep up the work you're doing, and don't ever go off the rail again, and I'm almost certain that you'll get your wish. Can you do that?"

Doug was finally catching on. "You're serious, right?" Mikey nodded in the affirmative.

"Mikey, I'd never let you down. Never."

"It's not about me, Doug. It's about you. That's who you can't let down."

Not another word was spoken as they made their way to the shelter, but Mikey could tell that Doug was trying his best to hold back the tears. "You can do this, Doug. I believe in you."

GERALD'S TURN

IKEY AND GERALD HAD butted heads right from the beginning, but their last outing was different, but in a good way.
They'd actually talked, and Gerald had let Mikey in just a
tad. But that might just be enough. Perhaps Mikey's heavy lifting was
beginning to pay off. "Before I get ahead of myself, I'd better see how
today goes." And with that, he pulled into the parking lot at the house.

It appeared that the Gerald of yesterday was back again today.
"That's a good sign." Mikey to himself as usual.

And then Gerald greeted him, and not with his customary grunt,
but an honest too goodness greeting. Like he meant it. "Beautiful day,
hey? I love this kind of weather."

"Ok, where's the real Gerald? Actually, I like this one better. Let's
keep him." Under his breath, of course. "Me too. Let's go down to the
boardwalk for a stroll. Ok with you?"

"You bet. Hey, do you really think someone would hire me? I
have a pretty sucky record."

Now we're starting to get somewhere. "Let me ask you a few questions, ok? Just answer me as honestly as you can. And don't get mad."
And with that, Mikey pumped Gerald for as much information as he
could. The more he knew Gerald, the better chance they'd have. Gerald
was game, and becoming more and more transparent with the passing
of the hours. Soon 2 hours became 4, and still he wanted to talk. And

dump. Mikey wasn't about to let this opportunity pass. When he finally dropped Gerald off, he knew as much about Gerald as Gerald did himself. "Yes, my friend, I think we can find someone to hire you."

JOLINE MAKES A DECISION

JOLINE HOLED UP IN PANAMA City for 3 days, phone off the entire time. But now it was time to get on with her life. Heading back to Seattle was definitely out of the question for the time being. "I love you all, but I'm not ready to talk to any of you. Sorry!" Besides, Joline could just talk to herself. Like now.

She hadn't been entirely comatose while here. She'd started to put together a few blogs that she'd been neglecting the last while, after all, that's where the bulk of her income came from. It was best she not shoot the golden goose.

Truth be known, she'd actually sent out 1 email. And last night, she'd received the reply. And now she was on her way to the airport to join her YWAM (youth with a mission) buddies in New Orleans for a couple of weeks. There's nothing like a mission trip to put everything into proper perspective. Besides, it was time for a reunion!

She'd sent an email to her Mom to let her know that everything was going great. "Say hi to Granny and Gramps for me. Love you. I'll call in a few days." That should do it for now. If need be, she'd hit repeat. Hopefully, she wouldn't have to.

DEREK CALLS ETHAN

DEREK KNEW THAT HE AND Claire's marriage was probably over. But he didn't expect it would end that morning. He thought they were just going to have a chat, and somewhere along the line he'd tell her about the detectives call. But that's not how it went, and Claire walked out of their life without a backwards glance. Apparently she'd been way ahead of him. He shivered as he recalled that morning. She was so clinical, so cold, so devoid of any humanity. Like he didn't exist. He shivered again.

But now as he wandered aimlessly through the house (it certainly wasn't a home anymore), he kept flashing back to the numerous times Claire had disappeared for days at a time, always with the excuse of being undercover. And how she could always turn on the charm when needed, to put his mind at ease. He'd always given her the benefit of the doubt, and even though some of her excuses seemed somewhat contrived, he trusted her. Isn't that what marriage is all about? But then the detective from Portland had called. Claire was under investigation.

What had he said? "I'm giving you a heads up. Professional courtesy. Talk to her. I'm sorry it has to be this way. I'll wait to hear from you."

That had been a few days ago. Derek had taken down his info. He'd better call the detective back. Professional courtesy and all. That's when Derek and Ethan arranged to meet. In Portland.

Derek had always loved road trips, especially since he'd gotten the convertible. Such a perfect time to think, and with the wind blowing through his hair, and the open road, what could be better? Besides, it was only a three hour trip.

"See you around 10 at the IHOP on 82nd Ave. You're buying." And with that arranged, Derek booked off the next day and headed for a meeting that would change his life forever.

These two had obviously checked each other out. It would turn out that they had crossed paths before but had never worked together. Both had spent much of their career in L.A. but in different divisions. Now, they'd been brought together in a way that would bind them in a way that neither would have suspected.

Ethan was already at the IHOP when Derek arrived. They greeted each other cordially, made some small talk, and then got down to it.

"I know she's your wife, but I'm not going to beat around the bush. Ok?" It might have seemed like Ethan was asking for permission to proceed, but he wasn't. He was proceeding regardless of any objections.

Derek wasn't taken aback. Not at all. "She's my ex wife. Let's get that straight."

Ethan nodded, then proceeded. " I believe Claire shot Richard. He's a piece of trash, and deserves it, but she should've finished the job. Now we've got a mess to clean up." He paused to give Derek a chance to speak.

Which Derek did. "I know you might not believe this, but I don't think Claire has even handled a gun. At least not around me. I don't buy it."

"Derek, have you ever checked her out?"

"Of course not. Why would I?"

"I'm sorry to be so insensitive, but there's a lot more to Claire than meets the eye. Did you know that she's under investigation by at least two police departments? And that she'd finally been let go by her paper because of suspicion of irregularities. In fact, several of the convictions obtained because of her evidence gathering are now under review, and a couple have been overturned." Again Ethan paused, awaiting a response from Derek.

Derek was stunned by what he was hearing. He'd never even considering checking her out. He had no reason to. But after listening to Ethan's diatribe, all those nagging doubts he'd experienced since known Claire were starting to surface. Could he have been that naive? Had he just seen what he wanted to see? And he'd shrugged off all of the mysterious absences. She had her reasons. He bought them. Simple as that. My God, he was a homicide detective used to people lying through their teeth. Why hadn't he questioned her more? But he knew why. He was in love. She was his wife. How dare he not trust her?

Ethan continued. "We can't prove anything. Richards not talking. The only reason we have her on our radar at all is because we had him under surveillance. He's a known pedophile. His favourite target is runaway kids, boys in particular. And that's what Claire nailed him on. He ended up in the system, lost everything, including his family. He deserved what he got but it turned out that Claire may have helped the evidence along a little. Just enough to put him away. He vowed revenge, and if my information is correct, he's already paid her a visit or two. You'd know about that, wouldn't you?"

Derek did. "I do. Someone planted a dead rat at our home. Claire was sure it was for her. I wasn't so sure. I've pissed off a lot of people in my day as well. And then someone cut my brake lines on my car, and I nearly had an accident. Again, I knew someone was after one of us. She was convinced it was her. You're telling me that it's this guy?"

"I'm almost positive. Did she tell you anything else?"

"She went berserk and started checking out recent paroles from cases she'd worked on. She was flying all over the country checking out various leads. But she did say she had to go to Portland. I never asked her who she was checking out. She's damn good at her job so I never thought much of it. Now I'm wondering what the hell else I've missed?" Derek was getting more irked by the moment.

"I'm sorry to drop this on you like this, but I thought it was better you hear it from me than to suddenly have the cops show up on your doorstep."

"You realize that she lives in L.A. now, don't you? Or at least as far as I know. I'm beginning to wonder what I know about anything any more." Derek was not a happy camper.

"Well, I might as well dump some more on you. This has nothing to do with this case. But it had a lot to do with you."

"With me?"

"Yep. It involves Claire, too, but it was one of your cases. Do you remember the Rodriquez case? About three years ago."

Derek was perplexed. "Rodriquez? Why isn't that ringing a bell? I never forget a case I've worked on."

Ethan interjected. "It was a cold case. Stayed that way for several years, and then, if my information is correct, there was a sudden break in the case. Apparently an investigative reporter stumbled on some new evidence that led directly to a suspect that had somehow slipped under the radar. It resulted in a conviction, in absentia, as the suspect had fled the country. At least that's what they thought. I'm surprised you don't remember the case."

"I'll look into as soon as I get back to Seattle. Seriously, it doesn't ring a bell. Obviously there's more."

Ethan continued. "The suspects family contacted me. It turns out that we had someone in common. My wife, actually. They weren't getting a lot of help, and even though I was in Portland by that time, I started doing some digging. And that's when I noticed some irregularities. As you know, these things take time, but about 6 months ago some new information came to light that would blow the case wide open. And that's when I knew for sure that the suspect had been set up. And I think by the reporter."

"You think Claire set him up?"

"Absolutely. I know it. But I'll need your help. And it's going to get nasty. I'm here to take down your wife. Sorry, man."

Derek was embarrassed. And pissed. But he'd need a lot more proof than what Ethan was offering up. And he'd definitely be talking to Claire. "Do you know where the suspect is?"

"I'm pretty sure I do. He made his way to Canada. I believe he's working in the oil patch in northern Alberta, somewhere around Peace River. Have you ever been up that way?"

"On several occasions, but mostly in the Jasper, Banff area, and I've stayed in Edmonton a couple of times."

"I think you and I need to take a trip to Alberta. Think about it. I'm going regardless, but since it was your case, I think you should come as well." Ethan was going to push this as far as he could.

Derek needed more information. "What do you expect to accomplish by going there?"

Ethan was ready for the question. "He's still on the run. His family has been unable to contact him. He needs to know that someone is working on his behalf. Well, that's me, and I hope, you. I need your help, man."

What more was there to say? The next several weeks were spent combing through every file Claire had access to. Nothing on Rodriquez. "But I'd better check with the rest of the department first before I tell Ethan to stick it." That turned out to be a good decision. There was indeed a file on Rodriquez, but it wasn't one of his. It had resulted in a conviction, as Ethan said, but then reopened when new evidence came to light. The suspect had indeed been pardoned, but had disappeared. And apparently the Feds were closing in on Claire as the prime suspect.

Derek couldn't deny the fact that Claire had access to a lot of department files, and if she had tampered with, or planted evidence, it was on him. "Crap! There's goes my job!"

So he called Ethan to tell him what little he knew. And that he'd arrange a chat with Claire. But they both knew that Derek had to get out in front of this mess or he'd soon be kicking pebbles on the beach.

CLAIRE FEELS THE HEAT

CLAIRE THOUGHT SHE WAS a pretty good chess player, but the game with Ethan was, at best, a draw. And now she was nervous. He seemed to know a whole lot more about her than he should have. "Claire, be careful around him. He's dangerous."

That's when Claire decided that she'd better visit her snitch again. Somebody had said something that led the cop to her. No one else knew anything. If he'd squeaked on her . . .

"We need to meet. Now! Here's the address." And with that she hung up. He knew something was amiss. They'd always met at the wharf. Not this time. He wasn't liking this one bit! He'd heard about the "shooting" just like everyone else. And when he heard the victim was the guy he'd been tailing, he knew this was going to get ugly.

So they met. She'd set up the time deliberately so she'd have time to scope out the place before the meet, and to ensure that she wasn't being tailed. That cop had gotten to her. And just in case her snitch was followed, she'd arranged a roof top view well ahead of their meet so she could watch his approach and any other activity that might be suspicious. She'd played this game many times before, and maybe she'd let her guard down during her dinner with Ethan, but that would never happen again. He arrived. She watched from on high for another 15 minutes. No suspicious activity anywhere. She had to laugh. The snitch looked downright nervous. Good. Now they'd meet.

"Why're you so nervous? Something I should know?" Claire was relentless.

"No. Everything's fine. Why are we meeting here? What's going on?" He wasn't liking this one bit. "This woman's nuts! I should've quit working for her long ago. Never again!" All to himself of course.

Claire ignored his questions but he dared not ignore hers. Finally, after hammering at the guy for what seemed to him to be an eternity, she let up. "Ok, I'm sorry, but I had to be sure about you. I need you to do something for me."

Crap! But what choice? "What do you need?"

So she told him and sent him on his way. She could hear him mumbling to himself as he headed down the street. "Big man. You really stood up to her, didn't you?"

That went well, at least in Claire's estimation. He hadn't been approached by anyone, of that she was certain. But that cop could be pretty intimidating. She'd laid it out clearly to the snitch. "If I ever hear that you're playing both sides, I'll take you down. I assume you understand exactly what I'm saying. Yes?"

He nodded in the affirmative. There, that was done. "Now, run along, little man." To herself.

CLAIRE ARRANGES TO PICK UP HER STUFF

C LAIRE DECIDED THAT IT was time to pick up the rest of her stuff and her vehicle. And say her official goodbyes to her parents and sister, and of course, Mikey. None of this would be fun but it was something she had to do. Not like before when she'd just walked away from everyone and everything. She had to shake her head at her own logic. "Claire, you're doing the exact same thing as before but this time you might have enough guts to at least say goodbye."

Claire definitely didn't want to see Derek, but there wasn't a whole lot she could do about that. So she'd suck it up. "Stay strong, Claire." And with that she boarded the plane for one last trip to Seattle, and a life she actually thought she could sustain. "What a joke! Who was I kidding?" And just for a moment she actually felt sorry for Derek.

It was early afternoon when Claire arrived in Seattle. Perfect timing. "Derek'll be at work so I should be able to slip in, grab my stuff and get out of there. I might not have to see him after all." She loved these one way conversations. So she caught a cab to the house. Weird. Her car sat out on the driveway, not in the garage where she'd left it. And it was full of her stuff. "Ok. What's going on here?" So she tried the door and her suspicions were confirmed. "Jerk!"

"You talking to me?" And there stood Derek. "I just thought I'd help you out. Everything's in the car. I thought you'd appreciate it."

She stared at him. She wasn't used to him standing up to her. So without a word she headed for her car. But Derek wasn't done yet. "We need to talk."

"I have nothing to say to you. Get out of my way." Claire was being Claire.

"You're being investigated."

That got her attention. "For what?"

"Quite a few things actually. The shooting in L.A. for one. And planting evidence in several other cases, apparently even some of my cases." Derek was enjoying every minute of this.

Claire's face went from flushed only moments before to a sickly paste. "I don't know what you're talking about. Are you nuts?" But she knew he wasn't.

And that's when he stoked the fire even further. "Ethan and I are looking into any files that you've worked on over the past several years, particularly mine. Shocked? Ethan and I go way back." Ok, so that wasn't quite the truth but it was sure fun watching her squirm for a change. "Derek, smarten up. Don't turn into a male Claire." He almost laughed out loud at the thought.

Claire never said another word. She abruptly turned around, got in her car and drove away. But still he stood in the driveway watching her. "You bastard! I hate you!" Nice Claire, nice.

So much for saying goodbye to her family. She cried as she drove. "I wanted to do the right thing. Thanks a lot, Derek." And without thinking she hit the gas even harder, and shot through the red light as if it wasn't even there. But it was, and so was the cop. She hadn't seen him but he'd seen her. When she glanced in the rear view mirror, she couldn't help but notice a very fast approaching vehicle with flashing lights coming up on her. She pulled over to let him pass, but he didn't. That's when it dawned on her that she was the target. "Crap! Now what?"

He soon let her know exactly what she'd done, and issued her a souvenir. All she could do was pound the hell out of the steering wheel. "I need to get out of here!" But finally Claire started to calm down. "Claire, get hold of yourself. They've got nothing on you." She decided to head back to the hotel lounge. A couple of drinks might do the trick. An hour later and Claire was back in control of her emotions.

A hot bath sealed the deal, and that's when Claire decided that she really did need to say her goodbyes. She'd just drop by her Mom and Dad's rather than call, otherwise the whole gang would end up there, and that could get ugly. So that's what she did. As usual they were delighted to see her, and deeply sadden by her decision to move to L.A. But as usual, non judgmental. How could anyone not love these two? She did, at least to the degree that she could love anyone. She pleaded with them not to call Janice. "I want to surprise her."

Janice was indeed surprised, and so was Mikey. She should've known that he'd be here. This would be a tougher sell. Three hours later she'd emerge still standing, but severely shaken. Again, they were unconditional. Sad, disappointed, but both still professed their love for her. She pulled out of the driveway, stopped at all the appropriate lights, and slowly made her way back to the hotel.

"I don't understand you people. After all I've done, how can you still love me? Why? I don't understand." Maybe she never would. And maybe her wounds went a lot deeper than anyone suspected, including herself.

UNCONDITIONAL LOVE

A T LEAST SHE'D DROPPED BY. And for Claire, that was a huge step. But still Mikey grieved her, a sister he barely knew, and yet in every way a prisoner as much as he'd ever been.

And now she was on the run again. To L.A. She'd returned yet again to the hole from which she'd escaped, this time voluntarily. She'd been vague about her intentions, possibly because she knew that he and Derek were close. She couldn't hide her disdain for Derek when his name came up, and that perplexed Mikey. He'd married these two. He and Janice had socialized with the two of them on many occasions, and when they were together, they acted as if they were newly weds. And suddenly it was over? It made no sense unless Claire was involved with someone else, and that seemed to be the farthest thing from her mind. Not that he'd know anyway. He wasn't exactly an expert on affairs of the heart.

Janice commiserated with Mikey. Her sister had walked back into her life, and her parents, after virtually disappearing for years. And now, less than three years later, she was once again walking out of their lives. It was strange. Claire expressed her love for all of them, but it seemed robotic. Like she didn't know how to love.

"Mikey, I wish there was something we could do. I feel so helpless. She's hurting, Mikey. I know it." Janice palpably felt Claire's pain.

He wrapped his arms around Janice and drew her close to him. "Janice, she knows we love her. She knows we'll always be here for her. We need to stay strong and we need to pray for her. She knows she can always come home." Janice knew he was right. She loved this man. And she mourned for his sister.

BE CAREFUL DEREK

EREK WOULD HAVE GIVEN anything to sit down with Claire for an hour or so, especially since she was in town. But he knew she'd be visiting her family this evening, and if he wanted to maintain a good relationship with them, he'd have to cool his jets. Besides, it'd look like he was on a personal vendetta, and that wouldn't do anyone any good.

So he waited until the next day before contacting her. That proved to be a wise decision. A good sleep can do that to you. And proper wording in a text can go a long ways. Within moments Claire responded. Yes, she'd like to meet.

Claire was just about to text Derek when his text came through. Perfect. He was coming to her, not her to him. Control freak? Just a little.

So they met. As professionals. Derek decided to tell her everything. He watched her reactions as he revealed more and more of his and Ethan's findings. She spoke not a word, but her demeanor spoke volumes. He wanted to hold her, to comfort her, despite her obvious deceit. "My God, she's my wife!"

Claire finally spoke. Of course, she denied it with what little vigor she still possessed. Derek's heart went out to her but he remained steadfast. And to himself. "Claire, give me something. Anything." But she didn't. And that saddened him. "I'll need to speak to you again by week's end. Ok?" She nodded. And that's where the conversation would end this day. Derek paid the bill and they walked out of the restaurant together. Neither spoke as Derek walked her to her waiting vehicle.

Claire sighed, and almost without thought, embraced Derek briefly, gave him a quick peck on the cheek, and headed down the street to her waiting vehicle. That's where she'd sit for the next half hour, head bowed over the steering wheel. Finally, she started the vehicle, signalled, and headed for the I-5. She'd make one stop somewhere along the way. An 18 hour non stop drive would not be on her agenda this day. But it would give her plenty of time to think.

Derek had a heavy day ahead of him, and he couldn't afford to be distracted, but that was nearly impossible. "Why, Claire? Why would you do that?" He went over it is his mind time and time again. And of course, he'd have to let Ethan in on their little chat. He liked the guy, and even though he and Claire were no more, he still resented his intrusion into their lives. But this was something that wouldn't go away on its own, so like it or not, he was part of it. Ethan was moving ahead with the file regardless. "You're in or you're out. It's up to you, but if you care for Claire at all, you'd best jump aboard." And he did care, so he did.

MIKEY'S CONFLICTED

IKEY HAD A FEW DISCUSSIONS with Derek since Claire left, but he felt that Derek was being less than forthcoming. That bothered him. They were close, or at least that's what he thought. And this was about his sister. "Come on Derek. I need to know what's going on." Mikey muttered to himself.

He and Janice were doing great. He'd even checked out a few rings. "Man, are they ever expensive!" Of course he didn't say that out loud in front of the merchant. He didn't want to appear cheap, after all. "Still!" He was pretty sure she'd say yes, but what if she didn't? Then what? So for now he'd just look. "Chicken!" Again, under his breath.

Mikey had tried to call Claire as well, but to no avail. She needed to know that he would be there every bit as much as she was there for him. They may not know each other very well, but they have a bond, and he would honour that unto death. "Claire, I'm coming to you."

But first, he needed to talk to Derek. He headed to the precinct. If Derek wouldn't come to him, then what choice did he have? He caught Derek just as he was heading out the door. "We gotta talk."

"Mikey, not here. I'll call you later. I promise." And with that Derek joined the other detective impatiently waiting by his car. Within moments they were gone, and Mikey found himself talking to the sea gull perched on the railing waiting for a handout.

"Fine. I'll see you tonight, Derek." The sea gull couldn't have cared less. And besides, he needed to meet up with Gerald anyway.

JOLINE CALLS MIKEY

JOLINE HAD TO ADMIT THAT she'd had a pretty good life. Spending the last couple of weeks in New Orleans with YYAM (youth with a mission) really brought that home to her. Being around Christ centred people who lived only to serve others always brought her back to defining her own purpose in life. She'd been fortunate to have a Mom, and grandparents, with such a strong belief system.

And now it was time to build her own home on that same rock solid foundation. She'd been fortunate to get established as a blogger at an early age, and that would continue to be one of her cornerstones. It provided a platform which made her a respectable living, and it gave her a voice that she fully intended to use.

But there were a few people she needed to consult first, starting with Mikey. So she called him from New Orleans. "Hi, its Joline. Is Mom with you?"

"Well hi! No, she's not. Did you try her cell?"

"No, I wanted to talk to you privately. Can you talk now?"

Now Mikey was getting concerned. "What's wrong, Joline? I'm alone. Go ahead."

With that invite, she did. For the next 20 minutes. She talked; he listened. And he agreed to not say a word to Janice. Finally they hung up, just in time as it turned out, as Janice, on impulse, decided to drop in on Mikey with coffee and some oh so yummy doughnuts.

Janice shook her head as Mikey elegantly delivered his sermon for her ears only. "There is a God, and he has delivered unto me a fair maiden, and manna from heaven. I am truly blessed."

How could she not love this crazy man? And how could he not love this crazy woman? And under his breath Mikey proclaimed to God and himself. "I'm going to ask her to marry me. I'm going to the jewellery store as soon as she leaves!"

Mikey was positively giddy. Janice was amused, but perplexed. "What's got into you?" And then. "Whatever it is, keep it. I love it."

"Cheers my dear." As they toasted one another with the still too hot coffee.

And he kept his promise to Joline.

DEREK AND MIKEY FINALLY MEET

"MIKEY, I'M SORRY IT'S TAKEN me so long to get back to you, but now I can tell you everything I know. I know I don't have to say this, but everything I'm about to tell you is strictly between you and me, ok?" Derek leaned over so only Mikey could hear him.

"Absolutely. Go ahead. You have my undivided attention." Obviously there was more to this story than Mikey knew.

"Let's put aside our personal situation for the time being, okay?" He didn't wait for a response. "Claire's in trouble. Big trouble. In fact, she will likely be charged with conspiracy to obstruct justice, and that could lead to jail time." Derek waited for that to sink in.

Mikey wasn't sitting on his hands on this one. "No way. She'd never do that! Come on, Derek, you know better than that!" He was getting peeved real fast.

"Calm down. Do you want me to continue or not?"

Mikey bit his lip and nodded. "Sorry."

"Mikey, There's a detective from Portland looking into Claire's past activities. He's convinced that's she's dirty, and it seems to have gotten personal somehow. That's the guy you saw waiting for me earlier today. If Claire is implicated in any way, then by association, so am I. I'm the one that gave her access to all my files, and once she's in my house, she could access any department she chose without arousing suspicion. Am I worried? You bet I am!"

"So you think she's guilty, don't you?" He spoke quietly. Mikey was trying to be calm, but arms tightly crossed over his chest suggested otherwise.

"Frankly, I don't know what to think. I've talked to Claire but she denied everything, of course. We're meeting again next week. I need her to come clean with me. I know you may not believe this, but I'm trying my best to help her. This isn't about me, Mikey. But she has to give me something to work with." Derek stopped to let that sink in.

"Derek, I'm sorry I got so uptight, but man, after what's she done for me, I'd die for her."

"Mikey, you'd die for anyone. Come on, we all know that!" Gotta lighten the mood somehow.

Mikey had to chuckle at that. "How can I help. I tried to call her but it just kept going to voice mail. I know she's avoiding me."

"You and everyone else. Listen, I want you to reach out to her. Go to L.A. if you have to. There's something else going on here, but I can't put my finger on it. Will you try?" Derek knew he was clutching at straws.

"Actually, that's what I was planning on doing anyway. I've already talked to Janice about it, and her advice was to just go and pound on her door until she lets you in. That's what she said. I agreed but I wanted to talk to you first."

"Well, at least we're on the same page now. You continue trying to get hold of her. I'll do the same, and I'll try and stall the Feds as long as I can. As long as Ethan (he's the detective) and I are working together, we still have time to figure this out, but if he thinks that I'm jacking him around, we're screwed. Right now, we're buddies, but that could change real fast."

"Thanks Derek. That answered a lot of my questions but I'm still puzzled over you and Claire. You're trying to save her from herself, even though you're split up?" Mikey was confused.

"I have to. Simple as that." What else was there to say?

GO FOR IT MIKEY

MIKEY WAS TORN. He wanted to head to L.A. immediately but that would be senseless. He'd have to be patient and keep calling or texting Claire. Surely to God she'd respond at some point. At least he had a better idea of what was going on. "Please Claire, let me in."

She had done so much for him. "I need this, baby sister." That's when he decided to head downtown to check out the jewellery store one last time. Then he'd make his decision. The moment he saw the ring he'd had them put on lay a way, any doubt he'd had vanished. So with the bravado of Sir Lancelot, he bravely slid his credit card towards the clerk, who had now become more of a friend than a clerk. She nodded her approval, rang it through, and joined him from behind the counter. She walked him to the door, they hugged as if old friends, and she sent him on his way. "She's a lucky girl! I wish it were me."

Now he was committed. And with each step he grew bolder. Thank God the vehicle was close by or he may have broke into a full out sprint. "Easy Mikey. Save your strength for tonight." He was downright giddy. When he'd calmed down somewhat, he texted Janice. He didn't dare call. She'd know in a heartbeat that something was up. "Can you meet me at Salty's tonight at 8? I'm in a meeting at the Church until 7:30 or so. My phone will be off but I'll check my texts when I can. See you later." That should do it. And then Mikey headed to the Church, for a meeting of one.

Fortunately there was never a shortage of work at the church, so Mikey was able to keep busy until the appointed hour. My God, was he nervous! Janice had responded in the affirmative within minutes of his text. At least he wouldn't have to cancel the reservation.

He'd arranged an intimate setting with the maitre'd complete with a dozen red roses, a bottle of their finest red wine, and then complete privacy for the next half hour. "Certainly sir. I will personally ensure that you are not disturbed." And then to himself. "And I'm quite sure that my exquisite service will be well rewarded."

All Janice could think about was the exquisite seafood that Salty's was known for. "You bet I'll meet you there. God, I love that man! I'm so blessed to have him in my life!"

Mikey always arrived early and this would be no exception. He wanted to see her face the moment the maitre'd brought her to their table. He didn't have to wait long. She practically glided into the room, every eye upon her, as she was led by the maitre'd to their special table. Mikey rose to embrace her, and then waited for the maitre'd to seat her. He slowed poured the wine, and then waited for Mikey's approval before continuing to pour the exquisite beverage into their waiting glasses. A moment later the roses arrived.

Janice was beginning to get it. "Oh my God, they're so beautiful! Ok, Mikey, what's going on?"

As if on que, the maitre'd took his leave. Mikey started to stammer, then took a deep breath, and continued. "Janice, the moment you came into my life, I knew you were my soul mate." He continued. " Janice, I love you more than life itself. I can't imagine my life without you in it." And finally, almost pleading. "Will you marry me?" And with that, Mikey got down on one knee, like he'd rehearsed a hundred times before, opened the ring box, which he'd been gripping for the last hour lest it suddenly grow feet and run away, and offered her his life.

She knew this was coming, and still she was unprepared. And hesitant; and for a brief moment Mikey thought he'd blown it. But then with tears streaming down her face, she allowed him to slip the ring on her finger. She stared at it for what seemed an eternity, and then she stood up, helped Mikey to his feet, and threw her arms around his neck.

"Absolutely! I thought you'd never ask!" And that's when the maitre'd made his appearance.

"Congratulations. Shall I bring the menu now, or would you like more time?"

Janice piped up. "Now please. I'm starved!" And they came back to earth.

Mikey could only sit and stare at this beautiful creature that would soon be his wife. And Janice thanked God, under her breath, for this wonderful man that he'd delivered into her life.

JANICE CALLS JOLINE

J ANICE WAS STILL ON cloud 9 when she finally arrived home after one of the most wonderful nights of her life. It was after 11, but she had to share the news with someone, and that first someone had to be Joline.

"Please, baby, answer the phone. Please!" Janice pleaded into the phone.

"Hi Mom, I was just about to call you. I have something to tell you, and I think you're going to like it!" Janice could tell that Joline was nearly as excited as she was.

"Honey, I don't want to be rude, but I've got some news as well. I need to tell you before I burst!"

Now that wasn't like her Mom. "You go first, Mom." She hadn't heard her Mom sound that excited for like, ever.

"Joline. Baby, Mikey and I are getting married! He proposed to me tonight. I had to tell you first." Janice blurted it out.

Joline could tell that her Mom was crying, but at least now they were happy tears, and she began to cry as well. So mother and daughter cried their way through the rest of the decidedly one way conversation for the next half hour.

"Mom, I'll tell you my news tomorrow, ok?"

"Oh God. I'm so sorry. I was so busy telling you about Mikey and me. Tell me now. Please."

But no. Joline wanted to wait until tomorrow. "Ok, Mom, I'll tell you this much for tonight. I'm coming home next week, and if it's ok, I'll stay with you for a few days. Then I'll tell you everything."

And of course it was ok. She didn't want to let Joline off the phone but she'd had more than enough excitement for one day. Next week would be perfect.

CLAIRE PUTS ON HER ARMOUR

LAIRE ALWAYS KNEW THAT one day she might slip up, and it appeared that day was now. Why did she have to shoot Richard? All she'd had to do was leak the evidence she'd dug up to a few of her sources, and watched the fireworks from the sideline. But no, she'd made it personal. Again. And now she was in trouble.

But one rule she adhered to religiously over the years was this: deny, deny, deny. Always deny. Never tell anyone. So what if you're their prime suspect? Make them prove their case. But don't give them any help. Stick to your guns and you'll be fine.

She had to admit that Ethan had unnerved her. He seemed to know a whole lot more than he should have. Especially about Eric. She remembered that case well, and sorry Derek, but I did take advantage of our relationship. But when I saw a file with Eric's name on it on your colleagues desk, I had to look. I'd tracked that piece of dirt for years and got nowhere. I had to look. And I got him. I had to fudge it a little but he would've gotten away otherwise. I had no choice. Claire went over it time and time again. "I did the right thing." To herself.

Claire didn't know until Ethan told her, that Eric's case had been overturned. She knew he was on the lam, but this could come back and bite her, and Derek as well, and that was never supposed to happen. Now Derek wanted to talk to her and he seemed to want to help her. "I don't understand. Why would he, after everything I've done to him?" Claire was confused.

She continued to systematically break the case down into bite size pieces. She'd do this until she found the evidence that they could possibly use to trip her up. Obviously it should be the evidence she'd planted, but she'd look at the case as if she were a new set of eyes looking for evidence of wrongdoing. Like they would.

Claire had tampered with evidence on three other occasions over the years, and each resulted in a conviction. Convictions that should have happened, but never would have, if she hadn't helped the cases along. And each perpetrator deserved what he got. In fact, each one should have been executed, and if she had her way, she'd be the executioner.

So she combed through all four cases methodically. Maybe they were coming for her but she wouldn't go down without a fight. And that was a guarantee.

That's when she noticed her phone vibrating amongst the stack of papers on her desk. She quickly answered it before she realized who it was. "Damn." But it was too late. "Hi Mikey. Sorry I didn't get back to you earlier. How are you brother?"

Mikey really hadn't expected her to answer so he was taken aback as well. "Hi. Glad I caught up to you." And now he had his opening. "I wanted to tell you the good news."

"Good news? Tell me." Now Claire was getting interested.

"Janice and I are getting married!" Mikey couldn't contain the excitement in his voice. "I asked her last night and she said yes! I had to let you know!"

"Mikey, I'm so happy for you. You've been through so much." Tears streaked down Claire's face as she shared her brother's obvious joy.

"Sis, I need to see you. I want to come to L.A. for a few days. It's important. Please don't say no." Mikey gritted his teeth expecting her rejection.

But that's not what he got. "I'd love that, Mikey. The sooner the better."

That he wasn't expecting. "Let's see, today's Wednesday. I could be there Friday afternoon, and maybe spend the weekend if that's ok with you?"

"I'll make sure it works. Call me with your schedule as soon as you have it, ok? And Mikey, I'm looking forward to it. Just you and me. Love you, big brother!" And with that, she hung up.

Her brother was coming for a visit. She couldn't have been happier. Her thoughts took her back to about age 8 when she and Mikey were actually happy. Because a year later, that all changed.

MIKEY CONTACTS DEREK

"**D**EREK, WE NEED TO MEET. Now, if possible." Mikey wasn't wasting any time.

"Sure. Usual place? 10 minutes. Bye"

Derek had long ago quit trying to figure out what the other party wanted to talk about. Let them talk. Then you'll know. Seemed like a good solution. But Mikey sounded really excited, and Derek had to admit, he was more than a little curious. So he ordered the coffee and waiting for his buddy to show up.

He could tell by the look on Mikey's face that whatever it was, it was big. And indeed it was. Derek couldn't have been happier for his friend. And Janice, of course.

But when Mikey opened up about his conversation with Claire, he really had Derek's attention. "Man, that's perfect! But Mikey, you'll have to be really careful. The last thing we want to do is scare her away."

"I can do this. She's my sister. I know she'll talk to me. And Derek, I'll tell her that you're on her side. Can I do that? You are, right?"

"Yeah, go ahead. Mikey. I'm been calling her as well but it's been ringing through to voice mail. Try and convince her to talk to me. It's really important. Tell her that I'll help her, but I need her help as well. And tell her to stay as far away from Ethan as possible."

They said their goodbyes. Derek headed back to the precinct, and Mikey headed to the church. It was time Pastor Rick knew that he'd have a wedding to perform in the near future.

Then he'd let Janice know that he was going to L.A. for a few days.

ETHAN MAKES THE ARRANGEMENTS

EREK HAD NO SOONER than got back to the office when Ethan called. "I'm just finalizing the trip to Canada. I assumed you're still coming so I went ahead and made the reservations. We leave Friday, and return to Seattle on the following Tuesday, maybe sooner if we find our man. That work for you?"

"Yep. Just send me the itinerary. I'm assuming you mean we leave Seattle on Friday, right?"

"You got it. By the way, have you been able to contact Claire? She's not taking my calls."

"Mine either. I think I'll leave her alone until I talk to your boy. Then I'll dig her up one way or another. See you Friday."

Derek knew he had some digging to do. But not on Claire. Not now. Ethan on the other hand . . .

So a rather interesting scenario was beginning to develop. Mikey was headed to L.A. on Friday, and he and Ethan were headed to Canada. On Friday as well. Derek could feel this thing coming to a head. But exactly whose head would roll was anyone's guess. All he knew for sure was that something was definitely amiss!

When Ethan got off the phone with Derek he knew something had changed. Derek was being way too agreeable, and that could spell trouble. He'd best be careful around him. One misstep and this could end badly.

MIKEY HEADS TO L.A.

JANICE COULDN'T HAVE been happier for Mikey. She knew he was grieving his sister's sudden move to L.A., and the breakup of her and Derek's marriage, but finally she'd let him back into her life.

So now he was rushing around, trying to get 5 days work done in the next day and a half. And of course, telling everyone he knew about their upcoming wedding. He was like a kid in a candy store! And yet, how could she blame him? His entire childhood had been stolen by the person who should have cared for him the most.

He even told Gerald and Doug about proposing to Janice, and furthermore, invited them to the wedding! These were his people after all.

And finally Friday arrived, and Mikey was on his way. Soon he'd be with his baby sister. And soon he'd understand her a whole lot more.

JANICE HEADS FOR THE BISTRO

J ANICE MAY HAVE SHAKEN her head at Mikey's antics after she'd accepted his proposal, but the truth was that she was just as excited as he was. And it was time to share it with Erin and Sylvia. Of course, Joline may have beat her to the punch, knowing her!

They were waiting for her when she arrived, and no, they hadn't heard from Joline for a couple of weeks. Perfect! Now Janice could fill them in on her and Joline's conversation as well.

But she'd decided before she'd arrived to postpone any discussion involving the rest of the family. That could wait until later.

PEACE RIVER, ALBERTA, CANADA

B Y THE TIME ETHAN AND Derek arrived in Peace River it was nearly 8 pm. They quickly checked into the Nova Inn, then Ethan headed down for a late dinner. Derek had apparently picked up a bug so decided to call it a day. Besides, he wanted to check in with Mikey when Ethan wasn't around.

Ethan couldn't believe his good luck. Derek was under the weather and had decided to stay in the room. Perfect! As for dinner? That was the excuse he needed to get some time alone. Within minutes of leaving the hotel, he and his contact were on the phone. They quickly arranged a meeting, and made the exchange. There's nothing that money can't buy, and that includes a hunting knife with a 12 inch blade, plus directions to where Eric was known to hang out.

Eric had made a fatal mistake when he threatened to expose The Ring if he was ever caught. Then he'd disappeared, and if it hadn't been for Richard's asinine need for revenge, and Claire's response to his threat, Ethan would've been no closer to finding him.

Eric wouldn't be the first person that Ethan had disposed of, not by a long shot. His role was to protect "the ring" at all costs. Ethan was very good at his job. And it certainly helped that he was an officer of the law. Finding out that Claire was married to a cop was the icing on the cake. So he'd befriend Derek, but he'd also remind him that Claire would likely end up in jail for planting false evidence.

It turned out that Eric was convicted, but in absentia, since he'd managed to slip out of the country. But Ethan had finally located him, thanks to Richard, and with Derek desperately trying to save Claire from prosecution, he had all the pieces of the puzzle he'd need.

Now he just had to ensure that he had an alibi himself. That's where his contact would come in. They'd meet about an hour from now at the pub, make sure they were loud enough to draw attention, and then Ethan would slip away, excuse intact, and take care of business. Then he'd slip back into the pub unnoticed, ensuring he'd have a solid alibi when, or if, it was required. Derek, on the other hand, was in his room, with no one to verify it. Perfect.

And that's how it went down. A body had been found in the back alley behind a rather well known establishment. No further information would be released at this time.

Time to ramp up the volume. That's when Ethan and Derek checked in at the local RCMP station. "Hi, I'm Ethan; this is Derek. I spoke with the desk sergeant yesterday." They both produced their passports and badges.

"Yes, that would be me. I'm afraid I have some bad news for you gentlemen. It seems your friend managed to end up dead sometime last night. Quite a coincidence, wouldn't you say?"

"Dead? Eric's dead?" Be careful not to overdo it Ethan.

That's when Derek knew he'd been set up. He didn't say a word.

The desk sergeant was no dummy. "Listen guys, he's at the coroners now. We'll know a lot more by tomorrow. I guess I shouldn't have to tell you, but I will anyway. Don't leave town."

"Of course. Do you have anyone in custody? Sorry, none of my business. Been a cop too long, I guess." Inside, Ethan was euphoric.

The desk sergeant wasn't buying it one bit. He'd be watching them closely until he had some answers.

Ethan and Derek walked silently back to their hotel. Derek was determined to stay calm, and he would, for now. He'd been set up, no question.

But Ethan didn't know the half of it.

CLAIRE AND MIKEY HAVE A CHAT

C LAIRE KNEW THAT MIKEY'S visit would be a watershed event for both of them. That is, if she had enough nerve to open the box. She dearly wanted to, but as cathartic as she knew it could be for her, it might be catastrophic for him. In fact, it probably would be. To herself. "I don't know if I can do it. Please, God, help me." Claire was not one to bring God into the picture very often. If God was so wonderful, then why would he let that awful person do what he did to her? And to the millions of other children each year?

"Damn right I'll bend a few rules if I have to, to put that scum away!" Claire burst into tears. She'd been doing that a lot lately. "Please God, give me the strength to tell Mikey everything. Please."

Mikey was excited to see Claire. He should have made more of an effort when she was in Seattle, but he thought he had all the time in the world. But then she left, suddenly, and it was too late. He'd be kicking himself for a long time over that screw up! Now he was on his way to L.A. to see his baby sister and hopefully talk some sense into her. But if he was wise, he'd let her do most of the talking.

Claire had insisted on picking him up from the airport. Resisting Claire was futile, so why fight it. Mikey made his way to the pickup area where he was greeted by the world's biggest smile. And then the world's best hug. "I love you, big brother!" Claire virtually radiated.

Mikey had expected another version of Claire to show up, but he'd take this one any time.

They made a quick stop to grab some grub, and headed back to Claire's place. They were both determined to keep it light the first night, but after a couple of hours it became obvious to both of them that they needed to put the niceties aside, and get down to business. So that's what they did.

This would end up being a long, exhausting night. There would be many shared tears, and there would be anger, and frustration, and grief beyond measure, expressed on this night. But they were in this together. And because of that, they just might get through this. Both of them. And finally, as the night surrendered to the dawn, they went to their respective rooms, exhausted beyond measure, but with a renewed hope that they would emerge triumphant.

MEANWHILE BACK IN SEATTLE

JOLINE DECIDED TO SURPRISE her Mom and show up a day ahead of schedule, much to Janice's delight. These two would never be lost for conversation, but Joline had a question for her Mom and she wanted an answer now. "So Mom, am I going to be the bridesmaid this time?"

"Hon, you can be whatever you want to be."

"Ok then, I want to be the main bridesmaid, not like last time." Oh oh, what was this all about?

Janice was taken aback. "I had no idea that you even wanted to be a bridesmaid last time. I just assumed that you wanted to be the photographer, and of course, singer. Why didn't you say something?"

"I just did. I'm sorry Mom, I shouldn't have brought it up. It's in the past." Maybe, but it had obviously been a sore spot with Joline.

Janice made a mental note to add this conversation to the "don't assume" file.

"Mom, let's go see Erin, ok? And then we can drop by Grammy and Gramps if that's alright with you." Joline was practically bumping off walls.

They arrived at the bistro at the perfect time. Erin had just passed off her duties to one of her staff, and she and Sylvia were about to go shopping when Janice and Joline arrived. Of course, hugs were in order, and the shopping excursion was put off for a couple of hours, and now these 4 could gossip to their heart's content, or share, or whatever 4 women do when they're together on a Saturday afternoon.

It turned out to be wonderful afternoon, but finally, it was time to go. Janice had called her parents to warn them of Joline and her dropping by a bit later. Of course, that resulted in them being invited for dinner. In fact, that's why Janice had called ahead. She knew her parents well, and any opportunity they had to break bread with their family, was a privilege they relished. And besides her Mom was an incredible cook.

ETHAN'S STORY EXPANDED

ETHAN KNEW THAT THE deal he'd made with the devil would bury him one day. But if he had his way, that wouldn't be anytime soon. He'd do the bidding of his masters until he was in a position to finally disappear, and not in the way that he made others disappear. He shook his head at the thought.

He'd lost his own family nearly 5 years ago. When his wife found out about his inclination for young girls, she kicked him to the curb. Ethan tried to explain, but how does one explain the inexplainable? He'd dealt with this his whole life, and he'd even taken it to God. "Please take these desires away from me. Please." But it didn't work.

He'd married, thinking that perhaps a normal life might keep his desires at bay. It worked well, for a time, and then the monster came calling, and eventually he succumbed once again. That's when he joined what was referred to loosely as The Ring. He was used to exploring the "dark web" as a detective, so it was relatively easy to hook up with others who shared his interests.

But it turned out others were watching him as well. They befriended him and soon he was theirs. His work as a detective could prove to be highly useful, if or when the Feds got too close. And soon he was in the disposal business. The Ring Ethan was associated with numbered in the thousands, among their numbers were judges, lawyers, doctors, many of the elite in our society, all with one common, ungodly denominator. And if anyone decided to go rouge, Ethan and his ilk were sent in to clean up the mess. Ethan was one of the best.

Claire had come dangerously close to exposing The Ring when she took down Eric. She knew what he was involved in, but was unable to nail him as a pedophile, so she took another route, and nailed him for money laundering. But somewhere between the court house and the cell that was to be his home for the next 3 years, he disappeared. Much to The Ring's chagrin. Had he made it to the big house, his life span would have been very short. But he had his own connections, and greased the right palms, and soon he was in the wind.

That made Eric incredibly dangerous. And it became Ethan's job to eliminate the threat. But Eric remained a ghost, that is, until the episode with Richard, another member of The Ring. And again, they were aware of Richards vendetta against Claire, and her response. So Ethan was sent to chat with Richard, a known associate of Eric's, and that's when the trail grew warm once again.

Richard knew he'd violated the code, but he had one ace left up his sleeve. He knew about Eric, and he knew they were looking for him. He could help but he needed the assurance of The Ring that they'd let him be. They did, and his descent into hell was all but assured.

"Sorry Eric, but better you than me." Richard shrugged it off, but he knew it was only a matter of time before he'd share the same fate. So he gave Ethan the only lead he'd require. When Ethan found out that Claire was married to a detective, and would do anything to defend her against the supposed charges being brought against her, he knew he could take Eric down, and Claire would go along for the ride. She'd taken down at least 4 of them over the past few years, and even though there'd been numerous attempts to take her out, she'd managed to survive. Not this time.

SATURDAY IN L.A.

ONCE CLAIRE OPENED UP, she didn't stop talking for the rest of the night. She talked about her life from her adoption onward. About never really fitting in, despite knowing that her adoptive family loved her dearly. And she talked about her college life, and how that had lead to a career in investigative reporting. And how she loved it, despite the danger involved. She talked about the incredible satisfaction she got from uncovering the dirt that permeated our society today. Claire went on and on about some of the cases she'd been involved in. And finally she talked about her incapacity to truly love anyone. "Mikey, I say the words, and I know that I mean them, but my heart feels like it's made of stone. "Mikey, you do know I love you, right?"

"Yes, of course I do. And you know that I love you. You don't question that, do you?" Mikey knew Claire was getting to the root issue, but he wouldn't push. He'd let her take as long as she needed, but he had a pretty good idea where this was headed. And when she got to that place, he'd be be there to help her through it. He and God.

Claire could barely speak through her tears, but she kept going. They both knew that the dam was about to burst, and both prepared themselves for that moment. Mikey was her safety line. He would save her. And finally she removed her finger from that last hole in the wall, and 25 years of pent up rage burst their final defence. Claire screamed as if possessed, and she hung on to Mikey for dear life, lest she drown. His tears joined hers, and finally she rested.

He propped a pillow under her head and then covered her with a blanket. She was completely drained, him, nearly so. He sat on the chair opposite her, tears flowing unabated. He knew she had more to tell him. In a couple of hours time, the cupboard would be laid bare. But for now, he needed a shower, and he needed to rest. And he needed to spend some time alone with God.

WE HAVE A VISITOR

JANICE BROUGHT IT UP FIRST. "Joline, you like making me suffer, don't you?"

"Mom! Why would you say that?" But of course she knew what her Mom was referring to. "Oh, you mean about my plans?" And she began to giggle. "I'm sorry, Mom, but I love watching you squirm! Love you, Mom!"

All Janice could do was shake her head. "You're such a brat!"

Joline took a deep breath, and was about to let her Mom in on her big secret when they heard the doorbell.

"Hold on. Probably just a salesman. Give me a minute."

Janice opened the door and there he stood.

"Hi Janice. Is Joline here?" Janice could only nod, and then caught herself.

"Joline, you have a visitor."

"Who even knows I'm here?" Joline to herself. She and her Mom stared at each other as they exchanged places. Her Mom seemed distraught. "Weird."

"Abbas! Hi. What're you doing here?" And then she apologized. "I'm sorry. I shouldn't said that. Come in."

"Joline. Can we go for a walk or something. I'd feel a little more comfortable."

"Of course. Give me a minute." And with that Joline closed the door gently, and informed her Mom that she'd be going out for awhile. "Mom, don't worry. I'll be fine." And with that she was gone.

"How'd you get here?"

"Cab."

"What if I wouldn't been here?"

"I made him wait until I knew you were here. Then I let him go. Joline, I had to see you in person. It's been driving me crazy!"

Joline wasn't going to make this easy. "I thought you made yourself completely clear. Obviously I wasn't that important to you. So I left."

Abbas knew he'd better tread lightly, or he'd be leaving Seattle real soon, and that was the last thing he wanted to happen. "I screwed up big time. Joline, I love you. This is driving me crazy. Please give me another chance. That's all I ask."

Joline wanted to tell him to get on the next plane out of Seattle, but she couldn't. My God, he'd come all the way to Seattle just hoping she'd see him! How flattering is that? And if he knew how much she still loved him, he'd be a whole lot less uptight that he was right now. But she wasn't about to let him off the hook that easily.

"Where're you staying?"

"I haven't got around to that yet. I needed to make sure that you'd at least see me. I wasn't even sure if you were in Seattle. I probably sent you a thousand texts, and dozens of phone calls without even one reply. That's when I decided I'd come to you, wherever you were. I couldn't just let you walk out of my life like that, not without trying everything." And then he was silent.

And that's when Joline took his hand, raised it to her lips, and kissed it ever so gently. "I'm glad you came. Seriously. But Abbas, I know where I want my life to go, and I'm pretty sure it's not the same direction as yours. But if you decide to stay for a few days, I'll definitely spend time with you. I'm not promising anything, but I have to admit, it sure is nice to see you again."

Abbas couldn't wipe the smile off his face. "Yes! Can you recommend a decent hotel, or hostel, something reasonable?"

Joline bit her tongue. Mom has lots of room but she didn't dare suggest that. For one thing, her Mom wasn't too impressed with Abbas, and secondly, she didn't want him knowing how happy she was that he'd gone to such lengths to find her. "God, I missed you!" To herself only.

So they walked back to her Mom's house. "Give me a minute." She and her Mom had a short chat, and Joline emerged, keys in hand. "Let's go." The Green Tortoise Hostel is close to the Pike Place Market and Chinatown. They're pretty cool places so it'll give us something to do while you're in town." Joline wasn't about to let him off easy. Forget that.

So they got Abbas settled in, and Joline promised that she'd meet him at the Hostel around 7 pm tonight. That seemed to satisfy Abbas, and it would give her a few hours to think, and hopefully pacify her rather anxious Mom.

WE HAVE A FINGERPRINT

THE NEXT COUPLE OF DAYS were decidedly awkward for both Derek and Ethan. Ethan could only speculate that someone must have got wind of their arrival and took Eric out before they could talk to him. "Maybe there's more to this than we know. Hopefully there's some DNA or something. Right now they think it's us." Derek merely nodded. "You're quieter than usual. Your stomach still bothering you?" Ethan was doing his best to keep the party going. Again, Derek nodded.

"I'm calling it a night. A good sleep might just do the trick. Night." And with that, Derek made his way back to his room.

The next morning the two of them were called down to the police station. "The autopsy's complete. Whoever did this was obviously a professional. The vic was stabbed to death. One entry point through the back, and into the heart, and it was over. He didn't even see it coming, if that's any consolation." The Sergeant paused, but then continued. "But we were able to life a fingerprint from the knife, and we were able to match it." And that's when he motioned two other officers into the room. "It belongs to one of you. Care to guess which one?" Then he waited.

Of course Ethan feigned disbelief. "There's no way! We've been together the whole time. Not a chance." Inside he was salivating.

Derek, as usual, didn't say a word.

"Officers, I'd like you to take our friend here into custody." He pointed directly at Ethan.

"What? That's impossible!" And then he glanced over at Derek. And he saw him smirk, and then he knew that he'd just been beat at his own game.

The Sergeant then turned his attention to Derek. "I have nothing to hold you on, but I know damn well you're involved. And you can guarantee I'll be letting your supervisor know! And one last thing, can I assume you'll be leaving our fair city sooner rather than later?"

Derek was only to happy to comply. "Yes sir, I'll be on the next flight."

That went even better than expected. Too bad Ethan hadn't done a better job checking Derek out. He just might have gotten away with murder if he had.

Derek desperately wanted to share his news with Claire. He picked up the phone, partially dialled her number, then hung up, time after time. "Damn! Just call her." But he didn't.

It turned out he didn't have to. She called him instead. "Derek, I'm so sorry. Please forgive me." Now that he wasn't expecting. "Derek, please talk to me."

"Claire, I have something to tell you. Ethan won't be bothering you anymore. He has nothing on you. And, Eric's dead."

"What? I don't understand. Where are you?"

"I'm still in Canada, but I'll be back in Seattle by tomorrow. Can you meet me in Seattle? It's important. And Claire, don't say a word to anyone until we talk."

"Yes I'll come. We'll both come, Mikey and me. Ok?"

"Yeah, that'd be great. How are you, Claire, seriously?"

"Derek, for the first time in my life, I think I'm going to be ok. I'm looking forward to seeing you. Mikey wants to talk to you. One sec." He could hear Mikey in the background.

"Hey Derek, sounds like you had a rough trip. You ok?"

I'm fine, but listen Mikey, you make sure you get Claire to Seattle in one piece, ok? I'm counting on you buddy. See you tomorrow." And with that Derek hung up.

He was no sooner done with that call when he received another. From the police station. "Oh great. What now?"

But this call was different. Ethan had requested that Derek come see him before he left town. He had some information for him. It was urgent.

Derek was curious. So he went. That conversation would not only change the lives of those closest to him, but of hundreds and perhaps thousands of others caught in a vicious cycle not of their own doing.

This conversation would not be videotaped, recorded, or bugged in any way, shape, or form. Derek would ensure that before one word was spoken. When he was completely satisfied, Ethan began to talk. And he started off by congratulating Derek on his victory. How could he not?

"Derek, I need to know how you did it? I had it all figured out, right down to planting your fingerprints on the knife. I had you, man. You and I both know that I'll never make it out of this prison. I'll be dead by tomorrow. Guaranteed. You give me this, and I'll give you The Ring. I mean it.

Why not? "It wasn't that hard really. I saw you slip my coffee cup into a baggie when you were in Seattle the first time. That's all I needed to know. So I checked you out, and I did the exact same thing. The only difference was that you thought you were smarter than me. Maybe you are, but that was your first screw up."

Ethan just shook his head. "Go on."

"It was pretty obvious to me that you weren't here to rescue Eric, but to take him out. You getting me involved to save Claire from prosecution was a pretty good move, but I know Claire pretty well, and I doubt she'd be that careless. I wasn't sure about that, but my gut told me to trust her, and to definitely not trust you. And why did you need me to go to Canada, really? All I could think of was that you needed a fall guy. That made sense. Me taking the fall to save Claire." Derek stopped to let that sink in.

"I'm impressed Derek. I thought I was good."

"And I wasn't under the weather either. But I still wasn't sure what you were up to, so I followed you when you left the hotel. By the way, I have photos of you and your contact." Ethan just shook his head. "And you know what happened after that. I let you plant your evidence, and as soon as you left, I wiped my fingerprints off and re-placed them with yours. Seemed like the right thing to do."

Ethan could only shake his head. "And then you waited for the other shoe to drop. I have to say I'm mighty impressed. You are good, I'll give you that." And that's when Ethan got serious. "Write every-thing down that I tell you. This is my gift to you and Claire, and maybe my only hope of not ending up in hell."

Derek wrote it all down, and then it was time to go. Ironically, in another life, they may have been friends, but definitely not in this life. Ethan had a couple more questions for Derek. "Do you believe in God?"

"Absolutely. Without question."

"Do you think I'm going to hell? That's probably a stupid ques-tion, isn't it?"

"If you go to hell, it's because you chose it. Tell you what, I'm going to drop you off a gift on my way out of town. Read the under-lined part carefully. Then it's up to you. Gotta go."

BACK IN SEATTLE

Mikey and Claire were waiting for Derek at the appointed location. Mikey gave Derek his usual bear hug, and then moved aside to give these two some space. It was awkward at first, but finally Claire went to Derek and wrapped her arms around his neck. That's how they stayed until Mikey broke the impasse by loudly announcing the arrival of their drinks.

After dinner they made their way to Mikey's. Claire would be staying here while she was in town anyway, so it only made sense. She had finally gotten up the courage to tell Mikey everything, and then at the last minute, she'd phoned Derek. And that changed everything. Now they were in Seattle. All three of them. It was time. She took a deep breath and began to talk.

"Mikey, I've been avoiding this my whole life, but I can't keep it inside any longer. Derek, I need to get this out. Do you mind?" He shook his head in the negative.

"Ok, you both know how obsessed I've been about all my cases, especially the ones involving children, right?" They nodded. "And you both know what a bitch I can be." Again, they both nodded. "That's not fair! That was supposed to be a joke." No joke Claire, if the shoe fits, wear it. So Claire carried on.

"Mikey, you went to jail to protect me, to keep me safe from our father, right?"

"He said he'd pick you as soon as you were ripe for picking. I couldn't let that happen, Claire. You were my baby sister." Tears welled up in Mikey's eyes as he recalled that scene of so very long ago.

Claire's eyes filled with tears but she gallantly carried on. "Mikey, you were too late. Two years too late. I couldn't tell you or Mom. He said he'd kill both of you. I'm sorry Mikey. You went to prison because of me." Claire could no longer contain her tears. Nor could Mikey. Or Derek.

She went on. "I wanted to die. He knew it but he told me if I told anyone or if I hurt myself, he'd carve you up right in front of me and mommy. That went on for two years. And then you shot him. And I remember hating you for it. You killed my dad. I was so screwed up."

Mikey went to his sister and held her as tightly as he could. Derek joined them. And now he was beginning to understand Claire. And she was beginning to understand herself a whole lot more.

But now it was Derek's turn. He pulled the notes from his breast pocket. A gift from Ethan for Claire, and for him, of course. And a hard drive with every name, number, and all the personal information of the members of The Ring, particularly the leadership.

Claire had taken down some of the members from time to time, but they were extremely well protected. And those who threatened to expose the ring soon disappeared. Most educated folk felt that the story of the ring was nothing but nonsense. How could something like that happen in our day and age?

Well, it does happen and it's happening now. A quick search on the Internet will confirm the above; an in depth search will convince you beyond any doubt that evil is alive and well throughout the world. And growing. Thank God for Claire, and others like her, that despite their horrific upbringing, became defenders of those least able to defend themselves, and became hunters of the monsters that lurk all around us. They're not all hiding in the shadows.

Maybe one is sitting next to you right now.

EPILOGUE

THE DARK WEB HAS ALWAYS been the place where monsters go to hide. Pedophiles are among the worst of them. The U.S. is not immune, in fact, there are thousands of members spread throughout the country. Their members include judges, police officers, teachers, scout guides, doctors, and so on. This particular ring is prevalent along the western seaboard and had operated for a very long time.

But now Derek and Claire had the information they'd need, and in the days and months to follow, hundreds of prominent members of this sick society would be arrested. Families would be destroyed. Businesses would suddenly fail. Suicides would increase substantially. And hundreds, if not thousands of kids would be given a second chance at life. Perhaps a good life, God willing.

Claire and Derek would become part of a task force who's sole purpose was to take down these types of organizations. And they would continue to work on their relationship.

Mikey and Janice would marry. She'd continue to write books. Living with Mikey, and having Claire and Derek in their lives, as well as Joline, ensured she'd have plenty of new materials for years to come.

Mikey's program would become a resounding success, but it would pit him against the street bosses in an all out war that threatened anyone who dared stand up to them.

Joline knew she had some big decisions to make. These were made far more difficult when Abbas showed up unexpectedly.

Ethan's prophesy came true as he had predicted. But in a final gesture, he arranged to have Derek's gift returned to him, with a few added pages that Derek and Claire might consider deciphering at a date of their choosing. And he added one rather interesting line of text. It simply said "I made my choice. Thank you."

And . . . Derek hadn't spoken with Millie for weeks. Truthfully, he hadn't even thought about her. "She must think I'm a real jerk!" That's when he decided to drop by her house. "Man up, Derek!" To himself.

He took a deep breath and rang the doorbell. No answer. As he glanced about, a vehicle pulled up, stopped, and the person emerged and put a sign on the lawn. For Sale. "Excuse me, do you know where Millie is? I'm a friend."

"She's moved back east. A sudden promotion or something, I think. Sorry, that's all I can say."

THE END

DD ANDER's BIO

D D ANDER never did fit in very well in the Prairie town he grew up in. While his classmates were settling down to careers and raising families, he was dreaming of mountain peaks and tall ships. And though he would attempt to follow these dreams, he would always end up back home on the prairies.

For a good part of his life he stayed the course, but eventually, he took his leave. He travelled extensively, and his experiences would soon catch up with his passion for a different life.

It would take him to places he should not have trod, and into experiences he should not have had. Stories would be told, by him, that he would deem fiction, but those who knew him, knew not where the fiction ended and the truth began. And they dared not ask.

He began to blog regularly during this time. Hundreds of blogs would follow, and to those who knew him well, it became obvious that the greater story lie between the lines. The public story was there for all the world to see, the other, for certain eyes only.

Although he lives in another part of the world today, he is always close by in one form or another. Whether through his blogs, photos, novels (fiction and non fiction), or one on one conversations, he is never very far away.

www. ddander.com

www.ingramcontent.com/pod-product-compliance
Lightning Source LLC
Chambersburg PA
CBHW071331250626
47159CB00004B/1558